MW01041350

Beautiful; Crazy

Eric Rickey

Shirley Jean Publications

Layout and design by Jennifer Cartright
Cover design by Michael Cartright

Shirley Jean Publications

ISBN 9798218510497

First Edition

Made in Missouri

For
Shelley and Morgan,
I love you

To Annie —
Thank you very much.
I hope you enjoy it!

[signature]

Table of Contents

THE INTRODUCTION 9

THE O'CONNORS'...11

THE MEETING 45

THE APPRENTICE 75

SPEECHLESS...91

THE ESCAPE 107

THE CONSEQUENCE.. 121

THE SECRET REVEALED 145

THE SEARCHING 167

THE CONFRONTATION..................................... 185

THE WAR... 209

THE VENGEANCE.. 225

THE EPILOGUE 251

Beautiful; Crazy

Chapter 1

The Introduction

My heart dances in my chest as I shift gears. Nervously, I pull a cigarette from the pouch and strike a match. I can't help but notice my hands are shaking uncontrollably. It's not fear that consumes me, it's anxiety. With each draw from the cigarette, I can feel myself starting to calm. I stare out the windshield, watching the beams graze the road. The hum of the engine, the rattle of the cargo I haul. It is intoxicating. I am alive and feel the anxiousness rise again. I know my life is forever changed......

Chapter 2

The O'Connors'

While sitting on a bench outside the general store, I move a rock back and forth across the brick of the sidewalk with my foot. As I notice the sole beginning to separate from my shoe, I lift it over my knee to get a better look. Peeling the sole back and staring at my big toe, I wiggle it back and forth a few times, observing the dirt caked in the creases. I wonder when the last time I bathed. The year is 1920 and I am only fourteen years old. My need for regular cleaning is not a top priority. Additionally, my parents died a few years back and my older brother Patrick is in charge now. He doesn't pay much attention to my hygiene, or lack thereof.

I put my foot back on the ground and stand up. As I yawn and stretch my arms out to the sky, I can feel my bones popping and it feels good. It's hot, as it usually is in the middle of August, and the heat is blistering, not even a faint puff of wind in the air. Sweat beads along my hairline and drips down my forehead and along the nape of my neck. I turn to look at my reflection in the glass of the general store window. My eyes are dark blue and hair dirty blonde, a little longer than I thought and mussed from not combing it. I see streaks of dirt on my forehead with crust in the creases. I'm already developing crow's feet from squinting too much and have small wrinkles on my forehead from constant scowling since I rarely smile. I find no joy in life and worry that I will never find anything to make me happy. I wear no shirt under my blue, overused overalls that are tattered and torn from running through the brush and briars. They've been patched a few times and look as if they need thrown in the garbage, but they're comfortable to me. While continuing to stare at my reflection, I lift my arm and flex my muscles. For my age, I have good muscle definition. I'm skinny but strong and tall for my age. I'm bigger than most of the other kids around town, and they fear me for it. I haven't been to school since my parents died due mostly to the fact that I have not said a word out loud since and most people think I'm simple minded. I'm not, I just don't have anything to say.

"Cieran, are you coming?"

I look up and realize my brother Patrick is waiting for me. He's holding bags of goods and has more sitting at his feet.

"I've been standing here watching you for at least a minute. You doin' some modeling for the folks inside?" he asks with a smile that stretches across his face.

He appears amused and stares at me fondly. Patrick O'Connor is the second oldest behind my brother Sean. He's a large man, not tall, but not short either. He has a barrel chest and huge arms. He always wears a white shirt and black vest that fits a little small, which I believe is to make him look even larger. He always stands out in a crowd. His hair is shaven up the side and a little longer on top that he keeps slicked back with grease. The facial hair is kept shaven, allowing him to flash a smile that melts hearts. His lip rises at first on the left side of his mouth, slowly exposing pearly white teeth and eventually opens wide enough to park a Buick. Unlike everyone else around town, Patrick never wears a hat. He just doesn't like them. Most people know Patrick as flamboyant and love him for it. He's witty, smart, and has an engaging personality. He's never short on conversation and always takes the time to ask about your day and seems to care when you answer. The thing I find most odd about my brother is that he wears boots like a cowboy with the bottom of his pant legs tucked in. We sold our horses a while back because we have money for automobiles and never messed with them very much anyway. I think my brother wears those boots simply for a place to hide his pistol. Patrick never goes anywhere without his pistol.

I pick up a bag of yeast, put it in the back, and climb into the front seat. Waiting for Patrick, I allow my mind to wander away from me. It is a beautiful day. If we hurry, I think to myself, I can still get to the hills and roam around. I am a person of solitude and spend most of my days and part of my nights exploring the hills around our house. After his death, I laid claim to my father's Winchester rifle and six shooter pistol. He taught all four of his kids how to shoot, and I am no exception. I'm as good a shot as anyone and able to kill rabbits, squirrels and any other animal that comes across my path. An Indian friend of our family, Crow, gave me a bone handle knife and taught me how to skin animals to butcher the meat. I am self-sufficient and able to take care of myself, for the most part. I spend as much of my time as I can in those hills hunting and exploring. I don't like being around people and do my best to stay away. The only exception is when I spy. I enjoy being able to sneak around houses and watch people without them knowing I'm there and if the opportunity presents itself, I will break into their house and steal from them. It's usually nothing major because people just don't have much. But I have stolen a few guns, bullets, jewelry and even a little money. I always get a rush from watching people and it's even better when I'm in their house walking around without them knowing. A few weeks ago, I got the courage up to walk around in one of our neighbors' house while they were asleep. That was exhilarating, and I felt more alive than ever before. I just sat around on their furniture and walked around their house while peeping in the rooms and watching them sleep.

My thoughts are pulled back when Patrick opens the door and slides behind the steering wheel. He starts the engine but just as quickly, shuts it off. I glance over at him to see what's the matter and notice Captain Lewis of the Joplin Police Department standing in front of our car. He's just standing there, hands in pockets, staring at my brother Patrick through the windshield. Captain Lewis is a man of small stature, short and skinny. He is always scowling and has wrinkles from his forehead to his chin from a life of it. He wears a handlebar mustache that turns at one end from his incessant gnarling. His hair is jet black under a dirty old fedora and wears a simple suit, hanging loosely from his skeleton. It must have been ordered directly from the J.C. Penney catalog; I believe. The only way to tell that he's a lawman is the badge he wears on his jacket pocket and the reputation that precedes him.

Captain Lewis stands there for a moment before slowly stretching his arms back and faking a yawn while walking to Patrick's side of the car. Leaning closer, he rests one arm on the door frame and pulls a partially chewed toothpick from his lips. "Pat, you've been ordering a lot of yeast lately," he says nonchalantly. "You happen to be running more than one still?"

Patrick smiles in the way that he does before passing a wad of money to the captain. "Just stocking up," he replies.

Captain Lewis takes the money from Patrick and puts it in his pocket without counting it. He stares blankly at Patrick for a moment before glancing over toward me on the passenger side. He is scowling through brown eyes that are dark and show no glimmer of love or life. Our eyes stay locked as he sucks on his teeth, creating a slurping sound that immediately irritates me. "Boy, you and your brothers better not be holding out on me," he says. "You better talk to old Pat here before he gets himself in trouble."

I sit there exchanging scowls with the captain, locked in eye contact and doing my best not to blink. He doesn't intimidate me like he does everyone else. I don't know why, I'm just not afraid of him. For that matter, I'm not afraid of anyone.

Patting Captain Lewis on the arm, Patrick quickly responds, "Don't worry, boss, you'll be taken care of."

Captain Lewis obviously doesn't like this as he quickly pulls his arm away while jerking his head lower and coming almost nose to nose with Patrick. "Dutch is looking for ya," he barks loudly. "Says he heard some things and wants to put it to bed. You know how he is, he don't want bad news to linger."

The smile disappears from Patrick's face as his eyebrows raise. "What's he heard?" he asks in a sinister tone.

The captain notices a change in Patrick's demeanor and visibly seems amused by it. He puts his hands on his hips and stretches his body backward, arching his back while lifting his head toward the sky. "Heard you boys are gearing up and not cutting him in," he answers. "Wants to make sure you still understand that he runs this town."

Patrick manages a quick smile, not nearly as comforting as normal. "You let Dutch know we're still good."

Captain Lewis leans back in the car window while grinning from ear to ear. "Let him know yourself," he says. "He wants to see you. Says you can come by the hotel tomorrow morning. Nine o'clock."

"I'll be there." Patrick replies quickly as he starts the engine and pulls away. I glance back and watch as Captain Lewis jumps backward to prevent his toes from being run over by the tires, and I sort of chuckle to myself.

I study Patrick as he shifts through gears and speeds out of town. He's mumbling something under his breath, and I can't help but notice how Captain Lewis has shaken him. I have never seen anyone get to him, and I am fairly certain that he isn't afraid of anyone. That's what makes him such a good bootlegger. He's tough and never hesitates to let people know when they cross a line. A quick punch is usually enough from Patrick, but I have seen him pull his pistol out of his boot and put it to the forehead of a few people when they fail to get the hint.

"Dutch." Patrick mutters as he shakes his head. He pulls a pack of cigarettes out of his pocket, fingers one out of the pouch, puts it in his lips and searches his pockets for matches. He pats all his pockets, moving from one to the other, but comes up empty. He continues to hold the unlit cigarette between his lips while he mumbles to himself, never moving his eyes from the road.

John "Dutch" Kelley is the leader of a gang in Joplin. He emigrated from Ireland and came out west with his brother, William. The two of them, using their natural gifts, developed a gang and strong armed their way into the mining industry where they made a fortune on zinc and lead. As the mines began to dry up and prohibition set in, they used their power and connections to solidify their position as bootleggers. Together, they took over and opened secret saloons, gambling houses, and brothels stretching through the entire county. The Kelleys' have their hands in everyone's pocket and ours is no exception. They are protected by the Joplin Police and are rumored to have a judge and Prohibition Agent on their payroll.

My father was an enforcer for the Kelley gang. He worked with Dutch to overpower the labor unions and keep the mines running strong. He was the common thread that kept the O'Connors' in the good graces of the Kelleys'. It's said that Dutch liked my dad more than his own son and even gave my dad his nickname, Mac. It's Gaelic for "son." Since his death a few years ago, the relationship between the Kelleys' and the O'Connors' has fallen a little downhill.

"We're going to stop off by the house for a minute and then we're going to check on Uncle Jack," Patrick says as he turns the car from the main road and off into our neighborhood.

We live in a neighborhood known to the locals as the Kansas City Bottoms. It's a small neighborhood made up of mining shanties mixed with a few updated houses about three miles north of town. Yards are unkempt and current amenities are rare. The roads are poorly maintained, and the area is surrounded by hills and heavily wooded. The community sprang up during the mining days and is known for having some of the roughest people in the area. All that live in this neighborhood are close knit but tend to stay out of each other's business. The police have to have a good reason for coming into our neighborhood, otherwise they keep out. You can't throw a rock in this neighborhood without hitting a moonshiner, and the bottoms are in an area that allows for this type of occupation to thrive. There are two dozen roads leading through the hills and twice as many foot trails.

Patrick pulls up in front of our house, shuts off the automobile, and steps out. "Wait here for me. I'll only be a minute," he says as he turns and trots toward the house.

I stare out the window and watch as Patrick scoots up the stairs and across the porch. He hesitates for a moment while seeming to think about something before he eventually opens the screen door and disappears inside. I let out a sigh and wipe the sweat from my forehead. I don't want to go to the hills. I know I'll be up there the rest of the day. My brothers and Uncle Jack have built a larger still that can brew four times the moonshine than other stills in the area. Patrick has been stocking up on supplies while also making new connections for distribution. All the moonshiners around this area run their product down to Oklahoma, but ole Uncle Jack makes the best around and we sell all of it to the Kelleys'. They use it in their saloons and don't want anyone else to get it. I always hear Patrick, and my brothers talk about trying to get away from the Kelleys' so they can make more money.

It's hot and I'm miserable sitting here, for what seems like an eternity, waiting for Patrick to return. I stare at the screen door for a moment before turning my gaze around the yard. This is not a happy place for me anymore and hasn't been since my parents died. I miss them awful bad. I can still picture my mom leaning on the porch rail, calling us for dinner. She was a beautiful woman and had a beautiful heart. She was loved by everyone and had a way of making them feel important. She was never short on conversation and seemed to go out of her way to help, always taking food to the less fortunate.

Both of my parents were killed in a fire at the house a few years back. It happened very early in the morning after Patrick took my brothers on an overnight hunting trip to the hills. My parents wouldn't let me go because I was too young to go without my father present. They say I was at home when they died, but I don't remember anything. My brothers came home to find our house burnt to the ground with our parents in it. It was a miracle that I wasn't killed with them. I was found a hundred feet from the house and had massive damage to my head, covered from one end of my body to the other with blood, and nobody knew how I got there or why. I was in the hospital for months and can't remember a thing. At first, I didn't even recognize my own brothers, but within a few days, I eventually remembered them. The doctors thought I was worse off than I really was, maybe brain damage that affected my speech or something like that, but I just decided not to talk anymore. I was broken-hearted from hearing the news of my parents and I've searched my memory ever since, trying dearly to remember what happened.

Dutch Kelley was the one who gave us the money to bury our parents and rebuild. Patrick and my brother Sean rebuilt the house twice as big as before, with enough room for the whole family. Patrick and his wife Sara share a room. There's a room for Ryan by himself, and a room for me and my brother Sean to share, although he rarely stays here. He's the oldest and, like me, doesn't talk much. Uncle Jack has a room out back by himself, says a bachelor must have his own place. I hate this house. It seems to take away all the memories of my parents, and I feel their presence fade with each passing day.

Patrick appears in the doorway, descends the stairs, and walks toward the car with two shotguns slung over his shoulder.

"Well, let's get a move on," he says as he opens the door and passes the shotguns to me. He's smiling again and I can't help but feel at ease around him.

Starting the engine, he backs out of the driveway and turns left toward the hills. We weave our way through the bottoms as I stare out the window, watching my neighbors as they move about in their yards, while rarely acknowledging our presence as we drive past. The ride is bumpy and my body jostles back and forth as

Patrick eventually passes through the bridge over Turkey Creek. Turkey Creek Bridge is an old, covered bridge constructed of wood years ago and serves as the unofficial boundary between the bottoms and the hills where the moonshiners hide their stills. Patrick slows as we enter the bridge and I watch while sunlight beams through broken boards and the bridge moans from the weight of our automobile crossing. Once through, the roads narrow and we take far too many right and left hand turns to count. In the days prior to Prohibition, my brothers and I would scour these hills for days on end. We know them like the back of our hand. Now I am the only O'Connor left that explores the hills since my brothers are too busy making moonshine. That's fine by me though. I don't want their company anyway.

After another few minutes, Patrick stops and backs the car into the mouth of a valley, where there's a large overgrowth of trees and bushes that allows the perfect hiding spot for an automobile. We climb out and unload the yeast, cornmeal, and sugar from the back. Patrick picks up some loose branches we keep around and places them along the front of the bumper to hide the automobile. He picks up the shotguns with one hand and a bag of yeast in the other. I scoop up the cornmeal and sugar before stumbling a bit as we set off on foot up the side of the hill. We follow a narrow foot trail up and around the side of the hill for another few minutes until we reach the mouth of a cave. Patrick drops the yeast, sits the shotguns on top, and stretches out. First reaching his arms to the sky before arching backward. He grips around his legs, leans forward, and almost touches his head to his knees. Now satisfied, he pulls a cigarette from his pack and offers me one. I lay my haul next to his and take it from him. Patrick strikes a match and lights his cigarette, then mine. We both stand there in silence, puffing on our cigarettes, and I catch Patrick smiling again. He's excited about growing our operation and it shows in his expression. Patrick has boasted to all of us that this would be our opportunity to make something of ourselves. He thinks this is our chance to make a lot of money and have everything we want. I can care less. I have no dreams of being an outlaw and want no part of bootlegging, no matter what it brings.

"Put your hands up!"

As I jump, I drop my cigarette and reach for one of the shotguns. Before I can grab it, two arms engrossed my body and pin my arms to my side. I squirm and grit my teeth but can't wiggle loose.

"Calm down, it's just Crow," says Patrick while grinning from ear to ear.

I feel his arms release me and I'm relieved to turn around and see our friend John Walker standing behind me with a smile on his face. John is a big man, tall and muscular. He has dark skin and dark hair, which he keeps long and is capped by a band worn around his forehead. He says it was owned by a revered medicine man from his tribe, most of whom are dead now. His Native American heritage can't be denied, as he wears it proudly on his face. He is best friends with Patrick, but we all feel as if he's part of our family. He's always been around since my father brought him home when he was a child.

"Where have you been?" asks Crow in a deep and raspy voice. "You were supposed to be here an hour ago."

Patrick lets out a sigh and shakes his head. "Got

held up a little," he answers. "Is everyone down there already?"

"Yeah, they got tired of waiting and fired up the still," Crow answers back. "You know Jack, he does what he wants, when he wants."

"What!" Patrick yells as he picks up one of the bags and sprints toward the cavern. "I told them to wait for me. I want to see it from the beginning."

Crow lets out a chuckle and pats me on the shoulder before grabbing the other bags as he turns to follow, leaving me with only the shotguns to carry. "Come on Cieran, we better get down there before Patrick loses it."

The opening to the cave is short but wide. All three of us have to get on our hands and knees to crawl through, dragging our haul with us. Just beyond the opening, it enlarges a bit and allows for enough room to stand on our feet. Even so, we have to hunker over and movement is slow. A foot or two inside the mouth of the cave, Crow and Patrick had built a mining cart and installed tracks, just like in the zinc mines. The two of them had found this cave in the days of their youth while they were out exploring and used it as their hangout. They stayed out here for weeks during hunting trips and even brought girls up here where they would smoke cigarettes, drink whiskey and all other sorts of bad behavior. This cave was where my brothers were staying when our parents were killed in the fire. I try not to think about that when I'm up here because I do like it. You'd have to be crazy not to, it's a neat place.

Patrick and Crow drop their packages in the cart and point for me to lay the shotguns on top. Once the load is secured, Patrick picks up the rope and pulls the cart behind him. I'm much smaller than them and I know I can make it through here faster than them, but I hang back a little. I find some sort of satisfaction as I watch as the two big men labor to make it through. The walk is slow. Other than the cart path, the rocks are jagged, with a few big enough to trip you if you're not paying attention. The path is lit only by daylight that peers in through the opening and shines down the tunnel and a single lantern that hangs on the wall about halfway down the tunnel. Crow snatches the lantern from the wall and holds it out in front of him as we move forward. Making our way down the shaft, smoke drifts into the glow of the lantern and I immediately recognize the smell of fire. It's pungent and burns my lungs with each breath, causing me to cough. I worry I'll pass out in the shaft and they'll shred the skin off of my body, pulling me out of here.

"This is why I wanted to be here," shouts Patrick. "They're going to kill themselves."

Patrick and Crow pick up the pace, cutting through the smoke and soon we are standing in front of a pair of makeshift doors. The doors are locked from the inside by using an oak log held by two brackets on each door.

"Open up!" He yells frantically while banging his fists on the doors.

A moment later, the doors spring open and out pops Uncle Jack. "Took you long enough," he says jokingly while grinning from ear to ear.

Patrick sighs deeply as he realizes the smoke has dissipated in the cave. The smoke in the shaft had been what lingered from the initial fire and wasn't able to escape through the cracks in the top. "I thought you all were dead," he says as he pulls the cart into the room.

I close the doors behind me and peer around. Twenty or thirty yards down the narrow shaft, the cave opens up into a giant room. The ceiling is over twenty feet tall, the cave walls are oblong and run a couple hundred feet in length and over a hundred feet wide. It's huge and encrusted with beautiful rock jutting out from all over. It's cool in here and two dozen lanterns light the room almost as bright as daylight. Back in the far end, my Uncle Jack had put his genius to use and built the most elaborate set of stills in this area. I am amazed by his handy work as he and Sean hammered out the sheets of copper for the enormous stills. On individual stands, he built four copper tanks, ten feet in length and connected by an intricate weave of tubing that lead to one large condenser fabricated of copper tubing engrossed in a copper pot. Most people use automobile radiators, but Uncle Jack says that causes lead poisoning and he won't put his name on a product that makes people sick. The cooling water is easily accessed from the brook that cuts through one wall and runs across the corner of the floor. I see my brother Sean kneeling by the condenser, busy filling jars with Uncle Jack's elixir and putting them into a crate. They have already filled five full crates and are currently working on the sixth.

"Why is he here?" Uncle Jack asks quizzically as he reaches out and pulls me in for a hug.

Uncle Jack is a big man. Not tall, just chubby. He's bigger than the drawings I see of Santa Claus and just as jolly. He always has rosy cheeks and a smile on his wrinkled, sun beaten face. He's missing a few teeth and the ones that remain are barely hanging on and tobacco stained. He wears overalls like me and a straw hat, just a dandy sight. He speaks with a deep voice that eccentrically elevates to higher volumes when delivering a punch line or while simply conveying one of his stories. Uncle Jack is funny, capable of entertaining anyone, and I can tell he genuinely loves me. I used to laugh at his jokes and stories when I was a kid, but I don't anymore, which seems to push him to always try harder to get me to laugh. Don't get me wrong, he never gets down on me for not talking. He's content with me just the way that I am and I think I love him even more for that. Sometimes, though, he talks to me like I'm a little kid and I don't care for that very much.

I can smell the alcohol on his breath and the smoke on his clothes as he holds me tight and musses my hair. Once again, he asks, "Why is the boy here?"

On his walk over to where Sean is busy collecting the brew and without looking back at Uncle Jack, he finally responds. "If we're gonna make more, we're gonna have to ship more, and that's gonna take all of us to get it done." Patrick kneels down, removes a jar from the crate and holds it up to the light. He smiles at Uncle Jack as he unscrews the lid. "Have you tried it?" Uncle Jack lets go of me and flashes a smile back at Patrick. "Yeah, I gave her a taste."

Patrick takes a swig and immediately begins coughing. Shaking his head and wiping his mouth, he passes the jar to Crow. "Wow, you've outdone yourself, big Jack!"

Crow glances at Patrick, nods his head, and tips the jar to his mouth. He doesn't take a small shot, instead he lifts it high and swallows half the jar. "Very good," he says while wiping his mouth before passing it back to Patrick.

Patrick takes another sip and tries to pass the jar

to Uncle Jack. "No thanks," he says while waving his hand. "I have my own." Uncle Jack walks over and flops down on a bed made of straw that the boys had constructed while up here camping. He lifts the edge of the blanket and pulls out a big jug, removes the cork and tilts it to the sky. "Come here, son," he says as he waves me over and pats the bed next to him for me to sit down.

I walk over and sit down next to Uncle Jack. He puts his arm around me and squeezes me tight. "I think you should be in school. Not down here fooling with us." He speaks slowly while turning his head to look at me and shaking it back and forth. "Don't you want to go to school?"

I stare back at him blankly, hoping he leaves it alone. I have no desire to be in school, nor do I have any desire to be down here with them. I simply want to be left alone to do as I please.

"He doesn't need school." Patrick interjects as he walks from still to still, inspecting Uncle Jack's handy work. "With the money we make here, he can do anything he wants."

"Well, I don't think he's cut out to be a bootlegger, he's too gentle." Uncle Jack replies with his arm still around me, but the smile gone from his face.

"Cieran let's move these crates down to the car," orders Patrick while ignoring Uncle Jack's comment. "I can make a shipment tonight."

Patrick picks up two crates and carries them over to the cart. As he sits them down, my brother Ryan opens the doors and pops out from the darkness of the shaft.

"'Bout time you got here." says Ryan while toting a shotgun in one hand and a jar of brew in the other.

Ryan is only two years older than I am, but not

much bigger. Like I said, I'm big for my age. We look almost like twins in appearance, but he is definitely different from me. He wants to be a gangster like in the picture shows and even dresses like them. He spends every dime he makes on suits and always chooses the flashiest. He has a personality like Patrick but is also known to be a hothead. He once beat up a kid in school for brushing against him when they passed each other. He loves the fact that we are bootleggers, and it appears to make him feel fifteen feet tall anytime he carries a gun. He always wanted to be a tough guy, like our father. Anytime someone tells a story about dad, Ryan always perks up listening intently. He smiles big and hangs on every word. I think it bothered him the most when dad died, although he never speaks about it.

Patrick glances up and sees the jar in his hand and snatches it from him. "What are you doing?"

"Just patrolling the area," Ryan answers while smirking, which causes me to immediately resent his attitude.

"Well, that stuff don't mix with guns." Patrick says as he playfully punches Ryan in the stomach. "Best keep your senses about you."

Ryan and Patrick are very close and always have been. Patrick takes Ryan to the show to watch the new gangster movies and totes him around town like a prize. Patrick knows Ryan looks up to him and I think it boosts his ego a little. When they were younger, it was rare to find Patrick without Ryan by his side.

"Help Cieran take this stuff to the car. You can be the lookout." Patrick says as he playfully gives Ryan a shove in the back.

After leaning the shotgun against a wall, Ryan

picks up a couple of cases of moonshine. "Come on, dummy." He says as he walks past the spot I am sitting. "Get a move on."

Ryan is always calling me names, and I don't like it. He's mean to me sometimes, even going back to when our parents were alive. I think mostly because I'm the youngest and he envies my relationship with everyone and the way they try to protect me. He doesn't scare me, though. I usually ignore him and eventually he shuts up and leaves me alone.

"Get up and help." Ryan jeers at me as he kicks my foot.

I jump to my feet and scowl at him, doing my best to let him know I am not afraid.

"What?" He asks as he sits the crate down and puts his face in front of mine with only an inch of air separating our noses.

I don't budge. While gritting my teeth, I ball up my fist and wait for him to make a move. If he touches me, I'm going to let him have it. This wasn't the first time he tried to bully me, and I've decided that I've had enough.

"Knock it off!" Patrick yells as he steps between us and pushes Ryan out of the way. "Sean, you help Cieran and Ryan can fill the jars."

Sitting the jar on the floor, Sean stands to his feet and walks over to where I am. "Come on Cieran, don't pay him no mind. He's just a bully." He says, while rubbing my arm.

Ryan puffs out his chest and scowls at Sean. "Why don't you just rock the baby to sleep, Sean?"

Spinning around and grabbing Ryan by the arm,

Sean tells him off. "Better watch your mouth before I put my fist in it."

Ryan wants nothing to do with Sean and drops his eyes. He's much taller and thicker than him, meaner too. Sean is the tallest in our family and has muscle definition even when standing still. His arms are long but chiseled and his torso is thick, even though he rarely eats and doesn't take care of himself. When it comes to fighting, no one can whip ole Sean, there is a darkness about him. He's the oldest and volunteered to fight for the allies during the war. He doesn't speak about it, but I heard stories about how gruesome some of the battles were. Now, he's just a simple man. He has dark hair that he rarely combs and whiskers that always seem a few days old, and I wonder if it grows that way. Sean dresses as a man much older than he is. He wears a simple shirt with trousers held up by suspenders. His face is weary and drawn at the mouth. Wrinkles cover his forehead and his hairline recedes a bit. Uncle Jack says it's because of what he had seen during the war, but never goes into detail. He drinks heavily and doesn't sleep very much. He is usually just coming home, as I am getting dressed each morning.

Wiggling loose from Sean's grasp, Ryan mumbles something as he walks away.

"Got something to say?" Sean asks as he starts off after him.

"Will you guys cut it out?" Patrick asks while he steps in front of Sean.

"Better tell him to keep his hands off the boy." Sean says aggressively while glaring down his nose at Patrick. "If I see it again, I will break him in half."

Patrick pats Sean on the shoulder. "I will," he says

calmly while trying to diffuse the situation. "There's no use in us fighting. We need to work together peacefully."

Sean stands there for a moment, still glaring at Patrick before finally relaxing a bit. He reaches down and picks up a couple of cases. "You, OK?" He asks as he walks toward me.

I shrug my shoulders and pick up a couple of cases. We both put our load in the cart and set off down the tracks. I'm much faster than Sean going through the shaft. I'm smaller and able to use my speed without having to lean over so far. I burst through the opening and scan the countryside. Not a soul in sight. I pull a cigarette out of my pocket and strike a match. The first inhale causes me to cough, since I have just recently started smoking after stealing a pack of cigarettes from one of the neighbors' houses. I'm not very good at it yet but I think it helps to calm me down though. I have a tendency to get anxious but don't know why. My body starts shaking and I feel like I can run a hundred miles. I am halfway through my cigarette before Sean finally pokes his head from the shaft, hesitating momentarily before climbing the rest of the way out.

"You got another one?" he asks as he stands to his feet and dusts his trousers off.

I nod my head and pass my pack to him. He takes one and musses my hair as he smiles. "You're a good boy," he says before striking a match and staring off into the hills. Seeming to get lost for a moment, the two of us stand there in silence while looking around and smoking our cigarettes. I like Sean. Because he doesn't say much and seems content to let me be, he also treats me good. "Well, come on," he says after flicking his cigarette into the brush. "They're not going to carry themselves."

It is a grueling trip down the pass to the car. I struggle to hold my cases as I watch Sean carry his with ease. I think about setting them down to catch my breath, but I don't want him to think I'm weak. Once we get to the automobile, we put the cases in the back and head straight back up the hill. When we arrive back at the cave, Sean picks up the last two cases before saying, "Go ahead and go back to the cave. I'll take these down."

I look into his eyes and shake my head. I pluck one of the cases from his arms and again head down the trail. Sean doesn't say anything, just shakes his head and grins as we once again make our trip to the car and back up again. I am just coming through the opening when I feel Sean grab a hold of me and lift me into the cart. "Sit still and I'll pull you," he insists. Shadows have fallen over his face, but I can still see he is smiling.

We enter the cave and find another four cases sitting by the entrance. I jump out of the cart and start putting them in.

"The still produces fast." Patrick says after walking over to help. "We only need ten cases for the first order. If they like it, they'll take more."

"The hardest part is carrying them from the cave to the car," Sean replies. "I think I will go to town tonight and get supplies to build another track to extend down the hill. Gonna need brakes too. Don't want the cart to get away from us." Sean walks to the straw bed and flops down where Uncle Jack had been seated. He reaches under the blanket, pulls out Uncle Jack's jug, and takes a swallow. "I might need some money."

Patrick turns and looks at him with a serious expression. "I need you and Crow with me tonight. I don't really trust these guys yet."

"But I thought you said I could go," shrieks Ryan from off in the distance. He notices how awkward he sounds and tries to regain his composure. "Besides, I'm a better talker than him."

Sean looks back at Ryan, unamused. "Let him go," he agrees. "I have other stuff to take care of, anyway."

Patrick thinks for a minute before responding. "OK, I don't think they'll try anything now, it's just a small order," he replies as he points his finger. "I guess you can ride down with us and bring the car back to get these two." He is pointing at Uncle Jack and me.

"That's fine," says Sean after taking another pull from the jug. "You think they'll be OK for half an hour by themselves?"

Patrick lays the last case in the cart and glances up at Sean. "I don't see why not. Uncle Jack can shoot and I'm pretty sure Cieran can too. Besides, who's gonna fool with em?"

Sean shrugs his shoulders and walks past Patrick up the shaft. Patrick watches him out the door and then turns his head to look at me before giving orders. "Take over for Ryan and make sure you listen to Uncle Jack. Don't drop anything and I will see you in the morning."

I walk over to where Ryan is kneeling and take the jar from his hand. With both our hands on the jar, he turns it sideways and let some of the moonshine pour out.

"Look," he jeers. "He's too stupid to even fill a jar!"

I look up and see Ryan grinning from ear to ear, showing how proud he is of the poor insult. I don't say anything and kneel to start filling. He must be satisfied with my lack of reaction since he turns and joins Crow on his walk to the shaft before the three of them disappear out of sight.

After a few minutes, Uncle Jack walks over and pats me on the shoulder. "Good job, my boy. You shouldn't pay Ryan any attention. He's just trying to get a rise out of you." I smile at him and watch as he waddles back to the straw bed and plops down. "Plenty more to make and times a wasting."

I watch curiously as Uncle Jack drinks from his jug. He is whistling a tune and seems amused by himself. I certainly find him amusing, but I can't figure out why he always has such high spirits. I am never in a good mood and always find myself thinking about the worst things. I can remember feeling joy when I was a kid, but that was before the accident, before the fire.

Uncle Jack is enjoying himself as I continue to fill jars. Soon, I realize my back aches and my fingers are stiff from turning the nozzle. I look around and find an old whiskey barrel Patrick had brought up here to hold water. Sitting beside the barrel is a table they had built and used to play cards on. I shut off the flow and pull the table close to the condenser. I struggle a bit to lift the condenser. It is bulky and almost tips over. I hook the table with my foot and scoot it under the condenser before sitting it down. As I walk over to retrieve the barrel, I notice Uncle Jack is looking at me peculiarly. His head is half-cocked to the side, and he is watching to see what I am doing. I roll the barrel over to the table and sit down before grabbing another jar and continue to fill.

"Haha!" Uncle Jack exclaims as he labors to his feet. "Bet ole Ryan wouldn't have figured that one out." He seems overjoyed as he stands up and walks to the still. I watch as he pours some yeast into a bucket, mixes in sugar and adds a little corn meal. He stirs and every so often, adds a little water. Uncle Jack is churning hard and is noticeably out of breath. After a short while, he climbs the ladder and adds a little to the tank, repeating the process on all four. With each dose, he hums a little tune and repeats the words, "a little drink for my babies."

We continue this process for hours. With every batch Uncle Jack makes, the drunker he gets. He is now shouting as he makes the mash and stumbles back and forth. I think to myself that he will surely fall into the fire, but he manages to avoid it somehow. He empties the bucket into the last still and pitches it against the wall. Turning around, he gives me a pat on the head. "That's it, my boy, we'll let her boil and call it a day." Uncle Jack is swaying back and forth, singing a jolly tune as he flops down on the straw bed. He reaches for his jug and clumsily rolls off, provoking a chuckle from me. Angrily, he manages to climb back to his feet and sways his way back to the bed, back to the jug. He leans over to pick it up and once again falls down. This time, he lands on the bed and that is where he stays. Passed out and snoring.

The last jar is taking a while to fill, and I figure there is not much left. I look at the fire, which has burned down and now gives only a few puffs of smoke. I glance back at the finished jars of moonshine I have stacked to the side, and I'm quite surprised to find that in only a few hours, we made twenty cases of Uncle Jack's finest. Uncle Jack has been asleep for an hour or so and still no sign of Sean. He was only supposed to be gone for thirty minutes, I think, and start to worry a bit. I get up and walk over to where Uncle Jack is sleeping and sit down beside him. I watch him for a minute before deciding to wake him. If I can get him up, we can walk home. I shake his arm, but he doesn't move. I shake him again, this time a little harder, and he swats me away as he mumbles something incoherently.

"Not going to do you any good. You have to be firm with the old man." Sean blurts out from the doorway, scaring me half to death. "He's good and drunk now, ain't he?"

I relax and nod as Sean walks over to one of the finished crates of moonshine. He pulls out a jar and takes a swallow. "Help me put the fires out and we'll head home."

The two of us pour water over the fires until we're sure they are out. I then watch as Sean walks over to Uncle Jack and shakes him violently. "Come on old man," He says as he pulls Jack to his feet. I run around the other side to help Sean get him stable and almost buckle under his weight.

"Let's get some dinner," Uncle Jack mumbles as we walk him to the cart. "I'm starving."

The two of us sit him in the cart and Sean hands Uncle Jack two jugs of moonshine. "Hold this and don't drink it all."

"Gladly," Uncle Jack replies, smiling widely as he pulls his feet up for easy transport.

Sean waits just outside the door while I extinguish all the lanterns before closing the door behind me. We're halfway up the shaft when Uncle Jack comes alive and starts singing an old Irish tune.

"Come back Paddy Reilly to Ballyjamesduff. Come home Paddy Reilly to me."

He's snorting and hollering while only singing the chorus. Over and over he repeats;

"Come back Paddy Reilly to Ballyjamesduff. Come home Paddy Reilly to me."

Slowly, we push Uncle Jack up the shaft, and it gets even slower getting him through the opening. I have to go through first and pull one end while Sean pushes from the other. With every inch, Uncle Jack screams and accuses us of trying to kill him. My patience is wearing thin and I'm not amused, but we finally get the big man through.

Uncle Jack barely makes it to his feet and peers down the hill. "Well boys, good luck with this." He is grinning from ear to ear and grabs us both around the waist with a jar in each hand and holding us loosely. "Let's give her a shot."

Sean looks at me, and sighs as we take off for the car. It's a grueling trip down the hill. With each step, Uncle Jack is wobbling and teetering on his feet. I'm not sure how we managed it, but eventually, we got him to the car and laid him in the back seat. Uncle Jack smiles as he sprawls out and pulls the top off a jar of moonshine. Again, he starts back up the singing, *"Come back Paddy Reilly to Ballyjamesduff. Come home Paddy Reilly to me."*

The ride home is slow but filled with jolly tunes. Sean now joins in on the chorus and drinks from a jar of his own. I am definitely not enjoying myself as much as they are and I'm sure it shows on my expression. The ride is bumpy, and Sean is driving faster than he should on these roads. You would think that he would recognize that I'm not having any fun as he rubs my head after each shot of Uncle Jack's magic elixir, but he doesn't.

"Come on ol' man," Sean says as he struggles to pull Uncle Jack from the automobile. We are home and I stand back, watching as Sean struggles to keep Uncle Jack steady. "I'm going to take Uncle Jack to his room. Make sure Sara brings him some dinner, OK?"

I nod and start up the steps to the house. As I reach for the screen door, I find Sara waiting for me with a plate of food already prepared for Uncle Jack. "Go ahead and take this to him, then you come in and get cleaned up. Your dinner is on the table."

I take the plate from Sara and nod in agreement. Sara was nice to me. She always makes sure I have food and takes good care of me. Sometimes, though, she tries too hard to get me to talk. She has a way of talking slowly to me and I know she thinks I'm stupid. She constantly sounds out words and tries hard to get me to repeat them. It drives me crazy, but she treats me good, so I tolerate it. I think she is very pretty, maybe even movie star pretty. She has long, black hair and a beautiful smile. Her lips curve perfectly and come together to form what appears to be a heart. Her green eyes sparkle, melting anyone who looks directly into them. She's very short and petite; probably not even a hundred pounds. Patrick dwarfs her when they stand next to one another. She talks almost in a whisper; except when she and Patrick fight. Boy was that a sight, her standing there looking up at Patrick with her finger pointed in the air, giving him the business. It works too. Patrick tries to argue for a moment, but always ends up agreeing with her. He usually scoops her up and holds her closely while they share a kiss. I think they're definitely in love, just like my parents. I fondly remembered my father serenading my mother with love tunes, no matter who was around. My mom would blush and swat at him, but you could tell that she loved it.

I arrive at the door of Uncle Jack's room just as Sean is coming back out. He takes the plate from me before saying. "I'm gonna sit with him for a minute and then I'm gonna take off. Don't wait up."

I stare at Sean for a moment before glancing down at his jug of whiskey. I worry about him all the time. He goes out drinking all the time and more times than I can count; he comes home bloody. Each time, he appears sad for a day or two. I don't worry about him fighting. I know he can handle himself, but I worry about someone not taking the beating well. I figure it's just a matter of time before someone shoots or stabs him.

Seeming to know what is going through my mind, Sean pats me on the head and smiles. "Don't worry. I'll be OK."

I stand there for another moment before eventually turning around and jogging toward the house. I spring up the steps and through the door. I go straight to the washroom and splash water across my face. Soaping up, I wash my hands and face before scrubbing my arms. When I get to the table, I see only one plate and know I'll be eating alone. I uncover my plate and find a generous portion of fried chicken, my favorite. I'm just biting into my first piece when Sara sits down and pats my arm.

"I knew it was only gonna be us tonight, so I made my famous fried chicken. Just for you." She says with a smile.

Sara is a good cook and fried chicken is her best dish. I never told her I thought so, but enough people had. I think she can tell I like it by the way I tear into it and the joy it brings to my face.

I give her a smile to let her know I appreciate the effort, and I feel she understands as she rubs my arm a couple more times before standing up and wiping off the table.

"I got you a special gift too," she said as she walks over to the counter. She pulls out a bottle of Coke and pops off the top. "Here you go. Don't drink it too fast or it will hurt your tummy."

This makes me happy, so I give her another smile. I want to reward her for her effort and hope she understands how much I appreciate it. I take a big bite of chicken and a drink from the Coke. Sara walks around the kitchen, moving about but not really doing much as I eat my dinner and we both remain in silence. I don't think she wants me to be by myself, but truly, I wish she would just go away. I swallow the last drink, making sure to get every drop before tossing the bottle in the trash. I walk over to the sink and prepare to wash my plate.

"Thank you, but I'll wash it for you." She says, while taking the plate from my hand. "Besides, what else do I have to do?"

I nod and turn to walk away.

"Good night, sweetheart." Sara mutters behind me.

I don't turn around; I just nod again as I cross the living room and head upstairs to my room. The house is large. It has two stories and is much bigger than the shack that used to be here. When it was rebuilt, it was fitted with electricity and indoor plumbing. We were the first to have it in the neighborhood. Dutch really did us well when he gave us the money to rebuild. No one really knew why he was so nice; we assumed it was due to how much he loved our father. We have all the new amenities. We have a full kitchen and living area downstairs, a study for my brother Patrick to do his business, and a washroom. I take the staircase up to where all the bedrooms are located. My brother Patrick and Sara share a master bedroom that has its own washroom and is big enough to take up half of the upstairs. Next to their room is Ryan's with mine and Sean's further down the hall. Across from our bedroom is another washroom, fit with a full tub. I open the door to my room and flick on the light. Our room is split square down the middle. My bed is on one side and Sean's on the other. My side is neat. I keep my bed made and my floor picked up. I always keep my stuff arranged neatly on the dresser and can easily tell if anyone touches it. Sean's side, on the other hand, is the direct opposite. He never makes his bed, and his stuff is scattered from one end to the other. Clothes are strewn across the floor and even cover his bed. He leaves moonshine jugs under the edge of his bed and across the floor. I leave his stuff alone, even though it drives me crazy. Every couple of weeks, Sara comes in and cleans it up for him. She gives him grief about it, but I think she actually likes it since she's always trying to take care of all of us.

I take off my overalls and fold them neatly over the foot of my bed. I can get another day out of them, I think as I open my dresser and pull out my pajamas. It's hot in my room so I open the window on my side of the room before walking over and opening the one on Sean's side, he won't mind. I stand in the middle of the room for a moment before thinking to myself that it was way too hot, and I would just sleep in my underwear. I put the pajamas back in my drawer before switching off the light. I lay down on my bed on top of the blankets, since there was no need for them tonight.

While laying on my bed and staring off into the darkness, I feel a sense of sadness wash over me. I close my eyes tightly and try to envision my mother. It has been getting tougher to do since her memory fades from my mind with each passing day. We had lost every picture in the fire, and I struggle to remember her details. There she is, I remember as I bring back memories of her auburn hair flowing in the breeze and the beautiful smile as it covers her face. I envision her holding my hands, spinning round and round. I am happy and feel her love in my heart while noticing that I am grinning ear to ear. In my mind, we keep spinning and spinning until eventually we both fall down. She holds me tight as she laughs, and I feel so comforted by her presence. I want her to speak to me, but I know she won't, she never does in my thoughts. I can't remember what her voice sounded like, and that hurts me worse than anything. I pull myself out of the memory with her and try to switch to my father. I can remember his stature better than his face. He was always serious and only smiled when he kissed my forehead following our prayers at night. That smile, however, was comforting and he would take his hand, brush my hair back and mouth the words, "I love you." All at once, my memory brought back my mother into the picture and we sat there, just the three of us, together. I love and miss them dearly. In a moment's notice, I fell fast asleep. Free from worries and hopelessly dreaming.

Chapter 3

The Meeting

I open my eyes, blink a few times to adjust to the morning sunshine as it gleams through the open window. My nose picks up a pleasant whiff of bacon frying, and I can hear slight laughter coming from downstairs. I stretch out in bed, allowing the bones to pop from my toes to my fingers. I roll over and see Sean sprawled out in his bed across the room. He is gently snoring, echoing only a slight buzz. I sit up and examine the floor. His clothes are strewn in a path from the door to his bed where his body must've given out and he was lying face down. I must have been exhausted, I think to myself, since I hadn't heard him come in. I stand and dress as quietly as possible, making sure not to wake him.

It's already warm in the room and I immediately become disappointed in myself because I had wanted to wake up early. I figured to be in the hills all day and hoped to beat everyone up and sneak out before they got around. I need some time to myself, and I have no desire to go back with Uncle Jack, though I assume that's where I'll be if they catch me before I get away.

I descend the stairs and cross the living room without making eye contact with anyone. They are engrossed in conversation and don't acknowledge my presence as I turn into the kitchen. There is no one around, so I make a beeline for the back door.

"Good morning," Sara says, popping out of the cellar door, stopping me dead in my tracks.

She pulls back a chair at the table, gesturing for me to sit down. "I made some bacon and biscuits, you want some jam?"

Sighing, I nod my head in agreement and sit down, realizing I am busted, and my escape will be tougher now. She places a plate in front of me. It's loaded with bacon and two biscuits, the sight of which is causing my stomach to growl, and I know it will be delicious. I cut the biscuits in half as she slides the jar of jam in front of my plate and slicks back my hair with her hand.

"You need a haircut," she says. "When you finish, we'll go out back and I'll trim it up for you, OK?"

I didn't acknowledge her; I went to work spreading jam and stacking bacon. It smells great and tastes even better. Sara was cleaning the kitchen as I eat my breakfast, and I am trying to come up with a plan on how to sneak out. I can hear conversation in the other room. My hearing is strong and I'm able to distinguish the voices of Patrick, Ryan, and Uncle Jack in conversation. They are having a good time as Uncle Jack tells them a story. He's always been very animated and has a way of engrossing your attention as he weaves his way through a story. Almost shouting as he delivers a perfectly timed punchline. I stop chewing long enough to pick up on the details of his story. It's about him and my father meeting with a local union organizer that was moving in on one of Dutch's mines. I have heard it many times. The two of them tied the man up and scared him so badly that he wet himself. Uncle Jack loved the part where the urine ran across the floor and my father was standing in it before they discovered he had messed himself. My dad was so mad that he had to walk outside. While he was out there, he took a hammer to the man's car, just for standing in his urine, not fully accepting that it was actually his fault and not the organizers. The union man was so afraid he immediately packed up and moved out of town, never to be heard from again.

"I'll take that," Sara says as she removes the empty plate from in front of me before putting it in the sink. "Give me a few minutes and we'll get that mop trimmed up. I bet you'll be a lot cooler without all that hair."

She's smiling as she picks up the jar of jam and screws on the lid. I feel comforted by her smile and truly appreciate the things she does for me, so I return her smile with a smile of my own. Her face lights up and I know I have made her day. Sara's lonely sometimes, and I know she wants a child of her own. She and Patrick have been unsuccessful, and I've heard her crying on many occasions, assuming they had failed in their current attempt. I assume she takes all her motherly desires and projects them on me. I appreciate that because my mother loved me so much and since she's been gone; I feel alone a lot. The love from Sara helps fill some of that void.

When she turns her back, I grab hold of the opportunity and slip out the back door with the last biscuit in hand. I descend the stairs and run to the shed as quickly as I can. I pull my rifle from the corner where I keep it hid under a pile of old clothes and search for my father's old satchel. I freeze as I hear footsteps come from behind and I turn to see Patrick step through the door.

"I need your help today," he says sternly as he takes the rifle from my hand. "Sara's gonna cut your hair, and then I want you to get cleaned up. We have something to talk about."

He was examining the gun, moving his hand along the barrel, feeling for flaws in its structure and not looking at me. I worry he will take it from me and keep it for himself since no one knows that I have a couple of dad's guns.

Without glancing up and remaining expressionless, he lays the gun back in the corner before turning to leave. "Come on, she's waiting on you."

I stand there for a moment, still thinking about running, but eventually I give up and decide the battle is futile. I would never intentionally disobey Patrick. I sigh as loudly as I can, but it's useless since Patrick has already disappeared and I know he doesn't care. As I turn, I flick the barrel of the gun with my finger and step out into the sunlight. Sara has already set a kitchen chair in the yard and is walking back into the house to retrieve her scissors. I run my hand through my hair, relenting a bit as I agree it needs a trim. Shorter hair will make me cooler; I think as I reason with myself and plop down in the chair.

Sara carefully steps off the porch and walks in my direction while humming a tune. I can see she is carrying scissors and a comb with one hand and a towel with the other. She's smiling, just as she always does. Coming to a halt in front of me, she wraps the towel around my neck. "Let's see if we can't make you a little more comfortable, huh?"

She walked around me a few times, leaning down after each pass and closing one eye as if she is sizing me up. "Well, first things first," she says. "I'm gonna have to wet it before I'm able to do anything with this rat's nest. I don't think you've combed it in years." Her attempt at comedy is useless and I don't smile, hoping she'll understand my discomfort.

She makes another trip back to the house momentarily before returning while carrying a bowl of water. She sits the bowl on my lap and pushes my hands up to clutch it as she dips the comb. I can feel my head being pulled with each motion of her arm. Repeatedly, she dips the comb and runs it through my hair. She groans with each snag as if she's struggling to pick a piano off the ground. I know she's doing it for my benefit while trying to ease my tension. When she is confident she has smoothed the entire mess, she drops the comb in the bowl of water, lifts the scissors to my scalp and begins to cut away.

As she cuts, she hums a hymn just as beautiful as a bird's song, pausing only long enough to check her work. I am lost in the serenity of the moment and let my mind wander to the days that my mother used to cut my hair. I think Sara is just as tender as my mother was, and I'm comforted by that. My mother wanted all her sons to look presentable and used to line us up every few weeks for a haircut. She was usually flexible and allowed my brothers to pick the style they wanted. As the youngest, she clipped my hair as short as she could without using a razor, and it seems as though Sara was taking a page from her book. I suppose she would have let me pick if I was willing to tell her what I wanted, but we both knew I wouldn't.

"Voila," she exclaims as she takes one final snip from just above my forehead. "Just as handsome as the day is long."

She removes the bowl from my hands as I stand up. I run my fingers through my freshly cut hair and notice she trimmed a lot. My hair is shorter than I am used to, but I can already feel the breeze blowing across my scalp and I know I will be much cooler with my new haircut.

"Is that gonna be, OK?" she asks as she wipes the loose hair from my forehead.

I nod in agreement, and she places her arm around my shoulders, leading me toward the house. "Good, now come inside and I'll draw you a bath."

I cock my head sideways and hesitate for a moment. Why did I need to take a bath if I was going to work all day I wonder?

Sara notices my hesitation and pulls me forward. "It's OK; you're going to town with Patrick. He bought you new clothes and everything. You're gonna be so handsome!"

I follow Sara upstairs and can't help but wonder what they have in store for me. Patrick rarely takes me along and I know he has a meeting with Dutch this morning. Surely, he wasn't making me go with him. What did I need to go for? Why doesn't he take Sean or even Ryan? I know he isn't allowed to take Crow. Dutch doesn't like Indians and won't allow them at any of his businesses. He rarely hires any to work in his mines, has to be hard up for help before he'll even consider it.

"Here you go, sweetie." Sara says as she pours a pot of boiling water into the already partly filled tub of water. "That'll keep it from freezing you to death."

She hands me a towel and a washcloth and starts for the door. "Put these clothes on when you're finished. Hope they fit." She pointed at a suit hung up on the back of the door as she closed it behind her.

I walked to the door and stared at the new duds. I've never had new clothes before, just hand-me-downs from my brothers. I rub my hand across the material on the trousers. It feels nice, not too expensive, I think, but not cheap either. I let out a sigh and wave my hand through the water. It's cool but not cold, so I undress and climb in. First, I splash water across my face, then lie back and dip my whole body. I pick up the bar soap and breathe it in. Jasmine, I believe. As I dunk the bar in the water and turn it over and over in my hand, the smell fills the air and before I know it, I'm lathered from one end of my body to the other. It's no use to fight Patrick on this, I think. Maybe, if I do what he wants, he will be satisfied, and I can slip away when we get back. It's easy to get along with him. He's usually busy doing his own thing and leaves me alone. I still can't figure his newfound interest in me. Why am I so popular all of a sudden? I don't want to be in the family business. I just want to be free. I enjoy being by myself. It's much easier than feeling the judgment people pass on me. Sure, they feel sorry for me, but I know they all think I'm stupid. I don't like most people and sometimes imagine myself doing bad things to them. One time, I overheard a group of kids talking about me and I waited down the street for them. As soon as they got close enough, I unloaded on them and pelted half of them with rocks before they knew what was going on. I would have gotten all of them, but they scattered and I had to get what I could. The others were still on my list and I know I'll get them.

"Cieran, get a move on," Patrick yells out from the other side of the door.

I splash water on my head and face to rinse the soap before climbing out of the tub. The water has turned gray from filth but carries a slight blue tint from the soap. I pull the plug and towel off. I finally recognize the clothes Patrick bought for me. They're styled after Bobby Jones and a lot of the kids around town are wearing clothes similar to these. The knickers are tan, short and tuck into black stockings just up the calf. They're wool woven and I think they wear heavy and probably too warm for this weather. I slide the shirt over both arms and rub it against my skin. It feels nice, like silk, but I don't think it is. The shirt is white and buttons down the middle. As I tuck it in my trousers and look at myself in the mirror, I can't help but admire the clothes. They fit like a glove, and I think I look pretty swell. I pick up the comb and run it through my new haircut, even though there isn't much left, still watching myself in the mirror. How did Patrick know what size to buy, I wonder? I put on my shoes with the sole falling off and realize they don't really match with my new look. Just as I am about to head out the door, I notice a tan hat sitting on the shelf. It's rounded with panels and has a button right on top. The bill barely sticks out further than my nose. I put it on and cock it just slightly to the right. Once again, I return to the mirror for a glance at my new style. Nice, I think to myself, even though I have no desire to dress up. I feel good in my new clothes. I look down in the mirror and lift my foot. My shoes are horrible and need repair, maybe even thrown away. They were passed down to me from Ryan and, lord knows; he got some use out of them, too. I place my foot back on the floor, turn and headed out the door, glancing back momentarily for one last look in the mirror.

"Very nice," Sara said, as I reach the bottom of the stairs. She hooks my shoulders with her arm and leads me on into the living room. "Let's go show Patrick how good he did."

We walk in and find Patrick, Ryan and Uncle Jack still sitting around talking. There's a small stack of money lying on the table in front of them. I dip my shoulder and break free from Sara, walk across the room, and take a seat in one of the empty chairs.

Patrick stands up and walks to a table by the door, retrieving a box that is resting on a table. As he is walking back over to me, I recognize that it's a pair of new shoes. I'm trying my best to keep a scowl on my face, but I am happy to be getting them. I just don't want everyone else to know that.

"The clothes fit well, let's see if the shoes do." He says as he places the box on my lap.

I wait a moment before pulling the top off the box. Everyone is looking at me and it makes me uncomfortable. I never liked being the center of attention, makes me uneasy.

"Well, try 'em on, lad." Uncle Jack blurts out before sipping on a cup of coffee.

I pull one shoe out to inspect. They are nice, white trim with tan leather around the toe. I untie my shoe and remove it. I look around and notice everyone still looking at me. I put on the new shoe and tie the laces. A little big but not too bad, I think, so I replace the one on the other foot and put my old shoes in the box.

"Do they fit?" Sara asks, taking the box from my hands.

I nod without lifting my eyes from my new shoes. I think they're nice, but I don't want anyone to know I like them. Sara seems to know as she stands in front of me for a minute before patting me on the shoulder and eventually carries the box out of the room.

"I don't see why he's going and not me." Ryan whines out from the chair next to me, causing me to look toward Patrick for an answer.

Patrick smiles at me as he stands up, ignoring Ryan. He plucks a few dollars from the pile on the table in front of him and walks over, passing it to me. "This is your share from yesterday's delivery. The more you do, the more you make."

I take the money from him and glance down to count it. I count two dollars, fold it up, and put it in my pocket. Patrick has never given me any money before. I have stolen some from our neighbors and keep it stashed in the shed out back. I think I have maybe five dollars total now. Maybe I'll buy something while I'm in town, I believe.

"Come on Patrick, let me go!" Ryan whines out again.

Patrick turns to face Ryan and shakes his head no. "I already explained this," he says. "We don't want to look too strong. Dutch knows something is up and I don't want you going in there trying to be tough. This is a delicate situation, and we all know he can make our life very difficult."

Ryan jumps from the chair and heads toward the door, stomping loudly and flailing his arms. "I'm not gonna do nothing and I think you should let me go instead of that dummy."

Ryan slams the door behind him, and Patrick shakes his head as he sighs loudly. "That's why you're not going." He yells toward the door that's already closed. Patrick stares at the door for a moment, then shakes it off and turns his gaze towards me once again. Looking me up and down and I think to myself that he's staring at me as if I'm a prized pig.

"You look nice," he says with a calmer tone and half a smile.

I scowl back at him and don't acknowledge his praise. I like the new clothes and the money. I just don't want anyone to know.

"I still don't like it," Uncle Jack says, cutting in. "I understand someone has to go with you to meet with Dutch, but I think the boy is too young. Hell, look at his face. He don't wanna go."

I glance at Uncle Jack and nod my head, trying to show him some appreciation. He's sitting on the sofa in the same clothes as yesterday. Only now, he's drinking a cup of coffee instead of his mountain brew. He gives me a wink before adding, "Wake Sean up and he can go with you. That way, if they try something, you'll have some help."

"They're not going to try anything. Dutch is a businessman and just wants more money." Patrick replies as he returns to the sofa next to Uncle Jack and begins counting money. He passes a little pile to Uncle Jack. "I already gave you your cut. This is Sean's make sure he gets it." He folds over a wad of money and stuffs it in the pocket of his vest. "This is for Dutch. That should make him feel better." He picks up the rest of the money and disappears to his office. Uncle Jack and I sit there in silence as I inspect my new shoes again. For some reason, that I don't understand, I like all the new clothes and shoes. I also like knowing I have a few dollars in my pocket. I don't know what I want to buy but I enjoy knowing I can if I want to.

After a few minutes, Patrick reappears into the living room. "Come on," He says, motioning for me while walking toward the door. "We're already running late."

Uncle Jack doesn't say anything else and I reluctantly get up from the chair and follow Patrick out the door and climb in the car. He sits down behind the wheel and starts the engine. As we pull out of the driveway, Patrick looks over and pats me on the shoulder. "I know you don't want to go, but I need you with me today. These guys need to see us as a simple family just trying to earn a living so they don't take all of our money."

Relaxing my face, I stopped scowling and sit there with a blank expression. Patrick has been building a larger still to do more business. I've heard him talking about how Prohibition is an opportunity for a man to make a fortune. In his mind, if a man has the fortitude, he can do anything he wants. I know the Kelleys' have us where they want. They get all the good moonshine from us to sell in their saloons and send the weaker stuff, which is inferior, down to Oklahoma. Patrick always says that Dutch is putting pressure on him to make more. Says they can sell all that we produce. Problem is, they just don't want to pay very much for it. Patrick talked to some people that are willing to pay four times as much as Dutch. I don't know why they're meeting this morning, but I'm fairly certain it's about money.

Patrick stops the car in front of the hotel and cuts off the engine. He pulls a cigarette from a pack, strikes a match and inhales deeply. As he reaches up to pull the cigarette from his lips, I can see that his hands are shaking and catch a glimmer of worry in his expression. He looks at me and notices that I'm staring at his hands. He lifts them slightly into his eyesight and watches for a moment as his fingers flutter. Ashamed, he quickly puts his hands down at his side, leaving the cigarette in his lips. After a few moments, he opens the door and steps out. I hesitate, allowing an opportunity for him to gain his composure before finally opening the car door.

As I step out onto the sidewalk, I stare up at the majestic Connor Hotel, the most exquisite place to stay in Joplin, and her beauty is unmistakable. At nine stories, I have to tilt my head all the way back to my neck to see the top. She's the tallest building in town, encrusted with beautiful Italian marble and ornate glass that is kept so clean; you can see the reflection of clouds and blue sky. As we head toward the entrance, we are shaded by a Roman canopy built of bronze and glass. Once we pass through the doors, a man dressed in hotel attire inspects our shoes to ensure they're clean enough to walk on the expensive carpet. Giant pillars of white Italian marble stretch from floor to the ceiling and seem to glow in the lobby's light. All around us, people are moving about. To the left is a barbershop which has every seat occupied, offering shaves and a haircut. To the right is the lobby and contains many people seated, reading a newspaper or engulfed in conversation. As we continue to the west end, we come upon the most elegant staircase I have encountered during my short life. We travel upward over marble steps and railings that are constructed from the same white marble as the pillars and are as equally impressive. Overhead, glass orbs are supported by bronze roses and illuminate the staircase. At the top, the stairway divides into opposing stairwells that lead up to a decorated parlor. We continue through the parlor and walk to the west end, where we find a set of double doors guarded by a large man wearing a suit.

"Patrick, how you been?" The man asks as we come to a stop in front of the doors.

"I've got no complaints." Patrick replies as he reaches out to shake the man's hand.

I've never seen this man before, but I see Patrick has. He's big and towers over Patrick. His hand engrosses Patrick's as they shake hands, and I catch a glimpse of a gun tucked into a holster under his jacket. The two of them exchange handshakes but never crack a smile, and I know they are not friends. Some professional courtesy, I believe.

"You know the routine," the man states as he feels down Patrick's side.

Patrick raises his hands in the air and allows the man to feel around him and even check the inside of his boots. "I'm clean." Patrick states once the man has finished.

The man nods and moves from Patrick to stand in front of me. "Gonna have to check the kid too," he says. "Sorry, just business."

Patrick looks over at me and gives me a reassuring nod. "He's just gonna check you for weapons. It'll only take a second."

I stand there silently while the man pats me down. He doesn't take as long with me as he had with

Patrick. Once finished, he steps back and opens the door. "Go ahead, they're waiting."

Patrick places his hand on my back and leads me through the doorway. Once through, it opens up into a beautifully decorated office. Straight in front of us sits a giant desk and behind that are two windows that look out over main street. Standing beside one window is another large man wearing the same suit as the man from the door. I can only assume that he's armed with a gun as well. Seated behind the desk is an older man that is shuffling through papers, and I recognize him immediately as Dutch Kelley.

As he stands and walks around from behind the desk, I can see that he has not changed a bit since the last time I saw him, which was quite a while back after I got out of the hospital. Dutch is a distinguished-looking gentleman and the black suit he is wearing seems to yell that he is made of money. He even wears a top hat and walks with a cane, which suits him. He is not a fat man, but not skinny and of average height. To see Dutch from a distance, he looks like an average person, but up close, his face seems to be formed entirely of stone and intimidates anyone that looks upon it. His gray hair protrudes from under his hat but is neatly trimmed. His beard is gray, neatly trimmed and encircles his mouth like a cloud of smoke. On the left side of his face is a scar that leads from his chin to his bushy gray eyebrows that are constantly drawn together in a scowl and cover his most dominant feature, his eyes. They are dark brown and hollow. My father used to say that Dutch has eyes straight from hell itself.

Dutch walks up to Patrick, extends his hand and, through a deep Irish accent, asks, "Pat, how ya been?" Patrick accepts Dutch's hand and, while managing a smile, he replies, "Just trying to feed my family."

Dutch stares at Patrick for a moment, seeming to size him up, and then withdraws his hand. "Aye, aren't we all?"

The two of them stand there eyeballing each other, neither of them moving, and I can't help but notice that Patrick is not his usual self. Normally, he would crack a joke or start telling a story with a smile crossing his face, but I have the feeling he is uneasy with this meeting. The uncomfortable silence lasts only a minute before Dutch turns and, while leaning down, starts examining me. Gazing up and down from head to toe before asking, "And how's my boy Cieran doing?"

He's talking to me but doesn't expect me to answer, which is clear when he glances back up at Patrick for a response.

"He's good," replies Patrick while shrugging his shoulders.

Dutch looks back down at me, reaching out his hand and pats my shoulder. "Good deal. He was always such a good boy."

I always liked Dutch but hearing him talk about me like that angers me a little bit. People had grown accustomed to talking about me, even when I was standing right in front of them. I give him a little scowl to show my disapproval and discomfort.

Dutch doesn't acknowledge my scowl. He just stands there looking me over for a moment, as if he is inspecting an injured horse before a race. He shakes his head slightly and stands back tall. "Come over and have a seat," he says. "My brother and son are on their way. Would you like something to drink while we wait?"

He is pointing to a table on the left side of the room. It's a large table and has enough room to sit another ten people. I follow Patrick to the far end of the table where he sits down at the head. I walk around him and take a seat with my back to the bookcase. I don't like sitting with my back to the door. It always makes me uneasy. "No thank you, we can't stay long." Patrick answers. "Too much to do."

"Aye, I am busy today as well." Dutch says as he walks to the opposite end of the table and sits down. He lifts the top off of a humidor and pulls out a cigar. "Would you like a cigar?" He asked as he pulls out a cutter and clips the end.

"No thanks," Patrick says as he folds his hands together and places them on the table in front of himself.

Dutch strikes a match and rolls the cigar around as he holds the flame to the end, puffing repeatedly. The smoke encircles his head as he shakes the match and discards the stick into the ash tray lying on the table. "All business, lad?" he asks with a partial smirk. "Surely you have time to enjoy some of the finer things in life."

Patrick doesn't answer, and Dutch doesn't seem to search for one. They sit there in silence with Patrick staring at his hands on the table and Dutch eyeing him closely. With each exhale of the cigar, smoke lifts and I can see the calculation in his eyes. Not once does he look in my direction and I can see that he is intently studying Patrick's movements, like a cat eyeing a mouse.

After a few silent and uncomfortable minutes, the door opens and in walks another old man that I know to be Dutch's brother William and a younger man, that I haven't seen before but think to myself that it must be his son. William Kelley is older than Dutch and it shows in the way he walks, stooping over and moving slowly. He's dressed as nicely as Dutch, but not able to carry himself as well. His face wears the wrinkles of time, and he is being helped to the table by Dutch's son.

I know Dutch has one son named Robert, though no one ever calls him that. Around town he is known by his childhood nickname, Bobby. Bobby Kelley is a smaller man, thin as a whip and has almost a gallop to his step. He is sharply dressed, wearing a pinstripe suit just as they wear in the gangster shows. He wears a matching fedora to cover his dark hair and a pencil-thin mustache just above his lip.

I can't take my eyes off of him as he helps William to his seat before lifting his head to look at Patrick. He stares only a moment before turning his eyes to me, at which time he stops dead in his tracks and appears as if he has seen a ghost. I am mesmerized by his expression and cannot remember ever seeing him before, yet he looks oddly familiar to me. I am staring intently at him while he looks back at me, mouth gaping and unable to speak. The two of us keep locked eyes, intertwined in a staring contest and neither blinking.

"Bobby, this is Patrick's brother Cieran." Dutch says as his words cut through the tension, bringing Bobby back to reality, where he quickly turns his head away and sits down.

As I search my memory, still perplexed by the familiarity of Bobby, I catch a glimpse of another man entering the room and turn my attention to him. This is a very large man, and he dresses similar to Bobby, except he's not wearing a fedora. His hair is blonde and combed perfectly to the side. His face is freshly shaven and his expression is as fierce as I have ever seen. The man walks over and stands behind Dutch. He then motions for the other guard, who is still standing by the window, to exit the room.

After everyone has settled in, Dutch stands and faces the man who had taken place behind him, whispering something in his ear. The man nods, walks over to Dutch's desk and retrieves a bottle of whiskey and four glasses.

Dutch turns back around and takes his place at the table. "Patrick, this is Evan Blake. He has joined us from our friends in Chicago and works close with Bobby to solidify this family's interests." He takes a moment before continuing, "I fully trust Evan and I want you to also, but if you don't, I will understand and I will ask him to stand outside."

The man known as Evan has returned to the table and is filling the four glasses with whiskey. Upon finishing, he walks to the end of the table and places a glass in front of Patrick before sitting the other three in front of the Kelleys'. Once finished, he returns to his position behind Dutch and put his arms behind him.

Patrick glances down at the glass of whiskey but doesn't pick it up. He lifts his head to look at Evan, then back at the now seated Dutch. Shrugging his shoulders, Patrick responds, "might as well let him stay. If you trust him, then so do I."

Dutch smiles and pushes the glass of whiskey to the side. "Good, now wait on the drink. We will share a drink once the deal is struck."

Patrick glances down at the glass and back up at Dutch with a quizzical expression covering his face. "What deal? I thought we already have a deal?"

"Don't play stupid," Bobby shouts as he jumps to his feet and leans over the table. "We know what you been up to."

My attention is immediately cast toward Bobby Kelley following his outburst. That voice, I have heard it before; I think. I stare at Bobby, searching my memory for something. I remembered hearing my father talk about Bobby when I was a kid, and I knew he hadn't liked him very much. He used to say that Bobby was a bad person; said this town was in trouble when he took over for Dutch and that he wouldn't work for Bobby Kelley. I know he had not been to our house with my dad, and I know my father wouldn't have taken me around someone he didn't like.

I am still watching Bobby and see as Dutch reaches over and grabs his arm. "Sit down, son. We're gonna get to the bottom of this. I'm sure Patrick wants to make things right."

Patrick is noticeably intimidated by the outburst, and the thought of being outnumbered. He is not as cocky as usual and seems to be thinking hard. After a moment and speaking in almost a whisper, he replies. "Bobby don't make a scene in front of my brother. He's not used to it."

Bobby eases up and sits back down in his chair. Smiling uncomfortably, he continues, "I didn't mean to get loud in front of the boy. Why don't we send him down to the lobby so he can get a soda, and we can get on with our business?"

Patrick shakes his head a moment before responding. "He's with me. I didn't come here to argue. I came here out of respect for Dutch."

Bobby is still grinning and I'm unable to shake the eerie feeling I have about him. His outburst makes me mad, and I can feel that I am now glaring at him. Since his entrance a few minutes earlier, Bobby hadn't looked in my direction a second time, but I haven't been able to take my eyes off him. I can see that he was peeking in my direction out of the corner of his eye and he seems very uneasy, almost upset by my presence.

William Kelley waves his hands in the air and speaks out in a very thick Irish accent that is fairly hard to understand. "We fix it."

Dutch takes this as an opportunity, patting his brother on the hand and speaking cautiously, "We have word that you have built a bigger still and are going to make more moonshine. We have also heard that you plan to sell it in Oklahoma and that you might have already made a trip down there."

Dutch's words clearly surprised Patrick and leans back in his chair, trying his best to remain calm. After taking a moment to gather his thoughts, he asks Dutch. "Who told you that?"

Dutch does not falter and quickly responds. "The same people you made your deal with are the same people we deal with every day." Placing his hands on the table in front of him, he leans forward and glares at Patrick. "Last night, you delivered your first load. We allowed them to buy it, only to send it back up here."

Patrick smiles uncomfortably as he realizes he's been caught. "Dutch, you don't pay enough," he replies cautiously. "This means more for my family. Now I understand you want your cut and I don't mind." Patrick reaches in his pocket and pulls a wad of money before tossing it on the table. "That's for you."

Evan Blake walks down to our end of the table and picks up the money. He quickly returns and passes it to Dutch, who takes only a moment to count it. "Twenty dollars," he says while chuckling aloud. "I could have made ten times that on the jars you sent down there."

"Yeah," Patrick responds. "But you would have only paid me a fourth of what they did."

The smile disappears from Dutch's face as he leans back in his chair and brings his hand to rest on his stomach. He reaches down and pulls out his pocket watch, clicks open the face, glances at the time and closes it. He's holding the watch in his hand while looking at Patrick and the silence is unbearable. After a few moments, he puts the watch back in his pocket and leans forward while speaking softly and says, "I will give you a dollar more per jar, but that's it and I want all you can make."

Patrick's expression does not change. He is stone faced as he weighs the offer from Dutch. "I will cut you a break, but a dollar is not enough," he counters. "I will sell you all that I produce for five dollars a jar. It saves me from having to drive so far to deliver."

Bobby laughs and my attention is once again snapped back in his direction. He looks like a goose squawking as he laughs, and I have an immediate hatred for him. There's something about him that just doesn't sit well with me. I can't put my finger on it, but I can sense it.

"I guess Patrick wants to run things." Bobby says while continuing to laugh.

Patrick sits upright in his chair, clearly not amused, before quickly responding, "I'm not trying to run anything, Bobby. I just want a bigger piece of the pie. You know there's nothing like our moonshine and you should pay for it. Why are you trying to rob us?"

Once again, Bobby jumps out of his chair and starts pounding his fist on the table. "Who do you think you are? I will have you both killed!"

I feel my face go flush as it starts burning and my heart picks up pace. I push my chair out and stand up. I can feel my chest pounding as I turn to face Bobby. He's standing on my side of the table, only a few feet away, and I know I can get to him before anyone stops me. If I'm quick, I think, I can tear his eye out with my thumb. That'll stop him from yelling at Patrick.

"Sit down, Bobby!" Dutch yells as he feels the tension swell.

Bobby appears surprised that Dutch is yelling at him and stands quietly for a moment, struggling to gain his composure. "I won't sit here and listen to this piece of trash. Tell us what he wants," he says, gritting his teeth. "He better show some respect, or I'll punish him for it."

"Relax," Dutch replies a little softer as he waves his hand at Bobby. "It's a negotiation."

Bobby seems to calm and sits back in his chair, leaning forward with both elbows on the table. All eyes in the room were affixed to Bobby, and they hadn't yet noticed that I was standing. My eyes are cutting daggers through Bobby Kelley, and I lose all recognition of time or presence. I want to hurt him. I can feel it in my soul, and I am really close to jumping at him before I feel Patrick's hand grab my arm.

"Cieran!" He whispered quietly.

I'm brought back to reality by Patrick's voice and notice that everyone in the room is now looking at me. Evan Blake has moved down the table in Patrick's direction and constantly stares at me intently. As I sit down, I glance back at Bobby Kelley. He is looking at me peculiarly, as if stunned by my action and not knowing what he should do.

Dutch Kelley stands to his feet and motions for Evan to return to his position by his side. "OK, let's get back on track," he states sternly. "Patrick, the only reason I don't squash you like a bug is because of the love that I had for your father."

I still glare at Bobby and watch as he snickers at the mention of my father. Once again, I can feel the anger welling up inside me and I want to attack him.

"I will give you three dollars per jar," Dutch says as he continued the conversation. "That's it. In closing this meeting, I will give you my word that you will continue to be protected from the Joplin Police Department and I will let you know that we have a new Prohibition Agent assigned to this area by the government and he is on my payroll. Without my protection, he will bury you and your family." He lifts his glass into the air and grins widely. "To the new deal and continued collaboration."

Dutch, William, and Bobby swallow the whiskey in their glass as Patrick sits there expressionless, staring only at the glass in front of him. "To the Kelleys'," he says as he finally raises his glass and swallows it whole. When finished, he turns the glass upside down on the table and stands to his feet. "The first delivery will be tomorrow, usual spot."

I stand with Patrick and the two of us walk out of the room. No other words are spoken, and I can't help but feel dissatisfied with my encounter with Bobby Kelley. I want, very much, to hurt him. The hatred I feel came from deep within my soul, and I can't figure out why. Had he done something to me as a kid? His face, his voice, both seem all too familiar as I search my memory for something to tell me why I disliked him.

Patrick was walking briskly, and I had to trot to catch up with him. Just as I reach the staircase, I stop dead in my tracks as I lay eyes on the most beautiful girl I have ever seen. She is walking across the lobby and appears to be moving in slow motion. Her white dress is flowing in the breeze created by her motion and is swooshing back and forth, hypnotizing me as she walks. Her auburn hair bounds with each step and shimmers as if she is an angel sent from heaven above. Her skin is milky white and appears to glow in the lobby's light. Luscious red lips mark her smile, which she displays to me as she passes by on the stairs. She has the most beautiful green eyes, and I know they have to be made of pure emerald. I am awestruck as she passes by and we hold our gaze for only a moment, still melting my heart. I watch as she strides up the stairs and walks directly to Bobby Kelley, who was standing at the door of the office we had just exited. I was horrified to hear her angelic voice utter the words, "Hello daddy."

Chapter 4

The Apprentice

The ride home is fairly peaceful as Patrick remains quiet the entire time and I sit there staring out the window, thinking about the meeting and, more precisely, Bobby Kelley. He bites his lip as he watches the road and never peers in my direction. Now, as we pull into the driveway, he appears to become agitated as he aggressively opens the door and climbs out. He doesn't wait for me and is already standing on the porch by the time I get out of the car. He is inside the house as I hit the porch, and I just barely step through the door when I hear his voice call out.

"Sean," He yells loudly. "Get up and come down here."

The others are gathering in the living room, and all continue to stand, except for Uncle Jack, who is sitting in his normal spot on the sofa.

"What happened?" asks Ryan, moving toward Patrick and looking worried.

Patrick shakes his head as he paces back and forth across the living room floor. I had thought about the meeting during the ride back from town. I had gone into it with no interest in the outcome, yet somehow, I feel entirely different now. I want to bury Bobby Kelley, and I hope to see Patrick stand up to Dutch. For some reason, I don't respect Patrick as much as I had before. I will never let anyone talk to me like that again, I think to myself. I have grown used to people talking down to me since I quit speaking, but now, after seeing the way Patrick looks, I am going to make sure they don't anymore.

Again, Ryan asks, "What happened?"

Patrick quit pacing, stopping still in his tracks. "They knew," he mumbles. "They knew about the delivery to Oklahoma last night. They knew before we ever went down there."

Ryan looks surprised as he stares at Patrick with his mouth gaping open.

Patrick continues, "And they threatened us. Pretty much said they get everything they want, or we die."

Sean finally arrives downstairs and walks to the sofa barefoot, shirtless, and looks barely alive. "What did you say to them?" He asks nonchalantly as he plops down next to Uncle Jack.

Patrick is glaring with his nostrils flared wide and starts pacing back and forth again. "I told them we wanted five dollars a jar and they could have as much as they wanted," he replies. "They said they would give three dollars. We'll just have to sell to someone else to make up the difference."

Sean reaches over and picks up a cigarette pouch off the table in front of him and puts one in his mouth. "Did you tell them no?" he asks.

Patrick glances over at me and then back at Sean. "I tried to, but they said they'd kill us."

Sean doesn't seem to hear him as he stuck a match and puffs on his cigarette. He looks tired and I wonder if he even knows what Patrick is saying.

"Let's get em all," Ryan shouts as he joins Patrick in his pace across the living room floor. "I'm not afraid of them. We have guns too."

Sean glances back up at Patrick. "Well, what do you wanna do now?"

Patrick stops pacing and addresses Sean directly, "We have to do what we have to do," he replies. "We'll increase the delivery to Dutch, but search for a place to sell the rest. How much do you think we can make?" he asks as he turned his head and looks toward Uncle Jack.

Uncle Jack takes a moment and gazes at the ceiling as if the answer is written there. "Thirty jars a day, maybe," he replies hesitantly.

Patrick nods before continuing. "We'll find someone else to sell to, but we will also have to find a way to get more supplies or Dutch will find out how much we are buying and figure it out. He's way too smart."

Uncle Jack smiles with approval and nods his head in agreement. "Whatever you want, my boy."

Ryan is doing his best tough guy impression as he is pacing back and forth across the room, just as Patrick had done. He walked over and stands next to me. "Let's just take over. I can kill Dutch," he says boastfully. "You should have taken me instead of this dummy and I would have killed em all." As he finishes the last sentence, he pokes me on the shoulder.

As soon as the words left his mouth, I feel my heartbeat pick up and my palms go sweaty. All at once, I swing my left hand backward and catch Ryan in the neck. His head tilts back, and he lets out a groan as I turn and fling my right fist into his eye socket. It's a direct hit and Ryan falls to the floor. I don't hesitate and jump down on top of him and swing away. Every shot was landing on the face of Ryan, and blood was dribbling from his nose. I'm lost in my anger and unloading on him. Years of abuse have finally welled up, and I am taking it all out on him. Ryan is screaming for help and scrambling for the door before I soon feel my body being jerked up from behind. On the ground, Ryan is writhing and covering his face as he lumbers to get to his feet before moving away.

"He's crazy!" Ryan shouts, as he wipes blood from his nose. "I didn't even do anything to him. We need to lock him up."

Still in a fit of rage, I struggle to get away as Sean and Patrick hold me back. I intend to show Ryan I am not a dummy and that he will not call me names anymore.

Ryan holds his nose as he walks out of the room before reappearing with a tissue. "He sucker punched me," he says aloud while trying to regain composure. "You all saw it. He's crazy."

Sean is still holding my arm as he replies, "maybe you shouldn't call him names."

"I'll kick his ass," Ryan responds while puffing out his chest.

Sean let go of my arm. "Kick it then," he says as he smiles wildly.

I lunge back at Ryan, but Patrick still has a hold of my other arm and we both fall to the floor. He's lying on top of me and no matter how hard I wiggle, I can't break free. "Calm down, Cieran!" He shouts. "Ryan, go outside for a minute!"

Ryan has moved away from me toward the door and is now standing with his hand on the door handle. "Why should I leave?" he asks as he wipes his nose and holds his eye with the other hand. "He's the one who is actin' crazy."

Patrick looks up and grits his teeth at Ryan. "Just go outside and calm down. We'll get him calmed down and then we all can sit down together."

Ryan appears disgusted but moves on through the door and stands on the porch. I can hear him mumbling, and I want to burst through and hit him again. Patrick is still lying on top of me, and I am feeling claustrophobic. I figure the harder I fight, the longer he's going to stay on top and hold me, so I give up and lay motionless under his weight. After a few moments, he takes the bait and rolls off of me.

"You calmed down?" He asks while lying on his back next to me.

I don't acknowledge him and climb to my feet. Looking around the room, I notice that Uncle Jack and Sean were sitting at opposite ends of the sofa and I move in their direction and take a seat in between them.

"'Bout time you stand up for yourself," Sean says as he pats me on my leg.

"Don't encourage him," replies Patrick as he lumbers to his feet. "They're gonna have to get along."

"Ryan's always pickin' at him," spouts Uncle Jack. "He's a menace and shouldn't fool with the boy. It's good to see Cieran knock the piss out of him."

Patrick walks over and takes a seat in a chair facing the sofa. Through shortened breaths, he responds, "I'll talk to him. We need to all work together to make sure this thing works. Uncle Jack, we have room for another still in the cave. If I get the material, how long would it take you to build it?"

Uncle Jack relents and again stares up at the ceiling, looking for the answer. He scratches the stubble on his face as he replies. "Two to three weeks, maybe shorter if I have some help."

Patrick looks over at me. "I think Cieran can help you down there every day," he says. "Bottling, running errands, or whatever you need. I would like to get to fifty jars a day."

Uncle Jack nods in agreement and wraps one of his arms around me. "I'll take the boy. He's a good hand."

Patrick continues, "Ryan, Sean, Crow and I will do the deliveries and help out when we can. First things first, we need to find a place to go with the rest. Any ideas?" he asks as he moves his attention toward Sean.

"Not really anyone that'll take more than a couple of jugs at a time." Sean replies.

I sit in silence on the sofa listening to them continue their conversation on where they can sell more moonshine. I've calmed down a bit, but still feel like I'm going to explode. My mind wanders back to the meeting with Dutch and I can't help but think about the girl I saw as we were leaving. She's beautiful and I want to see her again. I have never been interested in girls before, but now I can feel that I am in this one. I picture her curly red hair floating in the breeze. That beautiful smile she flashed me. What did it mean? Does she think I'm handsome, or was she just being polite? I imagine her speaking to me in that angelic voice. I can picture her resting her hand on my arm as she tells me a story. I imagine stealing a kiss as she pauses for a break, and I imagine her kissing me back. Can she really be Bobby Kelley's daughter? No way, I think to myself, she must be adopted. Maybe he found her somewhere and was holding her hostage. I will save her; I will be her hero and rescue her from Bobby Kelley and then she will love me forever. I'll have to find a way to see her again.

"I'm gonna take a trip to Kansas City and stay with our cousins. See if I can't find someone to buy from us, shouldn't be too hard since they know the players up there."

Patrick's voice cuts through my thoughts and I realize I must have been daydreaming for a while. Ryan had come back into the room and so had Crow. Crow was sitting in a chair next to Patrick and was watching him intently. I scan the room and notice that everyone is watching Patrick, so I focus my attention on him as well.

"When you going?" asks Sean.

Patrick thinks for a moment, "hopefully this afternoon," he replies. "I'm gonna go around and buy plenty of supplies and get materials for Uncle Jack to build that other still. I'll call the cousins and let them know I'm coming."

Sean nods in agreement. "You want me to go with you?"

"No," replies Patrick. "I need you to stay here and help Uncle Jack get everything set up. You'll also have to make a delivery to Dutch. They won't deal with Crow and Ryan is just too hot headed to do it."

"Hey," spouts Ryan. "I can handle it."

I can tell by Patrick's expression that he's not happy with Ryan, but he relents a bit. "You can go to Kansas City with me," he says. "That is if you can be good and promise not to start anymore trouble."

Ryan looks directly at me and squints his eyes. He's trying to intimidate me, but I notice his nose is bright red and his eye has already started to turn purple. Seeing this brings joy to my heart and I can't help but smile back at him, causing his cheeks to immediately turn red.

Ryan turns away from me and locks eyes with Patrick. "Yeah, I'll be good. You'll see that I can do this."

The conversation continued for a few more minutes and I listen as they work out the details of their plan. Patrick and Ryan are going to all the surrounding towns and stock up on ingredients. After that, they are going to get the supplies to build another still before taking off to Kansas City, Uncle Jack had told them where to find a man that used to work with him and my father back in the old days, told Patrick that the man runs a speakeasy up there and will probably take some himself and introduce them to others. It was also agreed that I'll help Uncle Jack and Crow will be the lookout man, like he usually is. Sean is going to help where he can and will make the deliveries to Dutch while Patrick is gone.

In the time before the meeting, I wanted nothing to do with my brother's business and just wanted to be left alone. But now, for some reason, I want to help and I want to see us beat the Kelleys'. I imagine my brother Patrick grabbing Bobby by his skinny neck and snapping it in two. I know the Kelleys' are strong and Dutch hires the toughest guys. Evan Blake is one of them. I can see that he's a serious man and is probably as tough as anybody. They have us outnumbered and outgunned, but I think to myself that there's always a way to get what you want. You just have to be willing to take it.

Back at the cave, Sean is busy building a railing system that runs from where we park the car on up to the opening of the cavern. I overheard him telling Uncle Jack that he had stolen the materials from one of Dutch's mines; they both got a kick out of that. Inside, Uncle Jack is preparing his still and I'm helping.

"First things first," he says. "We have to start the fires. Now you don't want them too hot at first, so we'll only put a few logs on."

I watch as he places four logs under the first still and then I do the same for the second and third while he does the fourth.

"Good," he says while patting me on the back. "Now we don't want to take too long building a fire, so we'll give it a little helping hand."

He walks over to one of the crates we had finished the night before and pulls out a jar. While returning to the first still, he pulls the top from the jar and takes a swallow.

"That'll do." He says, smiling proudly before pouring a dose on the wood. He hands me the jar and points down the row of tanks. "Now make a trail from this one that runs across the other three."

I walk over and pour the moonshine in a trail from the wood under the first still across the second, third, and then the fourth. When finished, I hand the jar back to Uncle Jack and watch as he takes another swig. He cocks his head to the side, groans a little, and then takes another.

"It's not a good idea to mix the two," he says as he sits the jar on the floor. "You'll burn yourself up."

Uncle Jack is grinning wildly as he lights a match and throws it on the wood under the first still. Bewildered, I watch as it burst into flames and follows the path of the moonshine, lighting each still all the way down the line.

"Now we'll let 'em heat up a bit." He says as he picks up a bucket and carries it over to where the bags of ingredients are sitting. He sits the bucket down and measures out some yeast and pours it into the bucket. I watch intently as he does the same with sugar, malted barley, and cornmeal. He hands me a stick, "stir that up, will ya?" As I mix the powder, he slowly pours in water. At first, the mixture is thick and I'm straining to churn it, however, after a few minutes it transforms into fluid and is easily mixed.

Uncle Jack walks over and picks up a ladder that has been lying next to the wall. He positioned it up the side of the first still and pointed for me to climb. "Pour that in and don't drop the bucket."

As I climb to the top and empty the bucket, I catch Uncle Jack stealing another drink of moonshine. He must be feeling it, I think as he's humming a little tune and soon, he will be in full song.

Uncle Jack meets me at the bottom of the ladder and pats me on the back. "Good, now that's called a mash. We'll do that for all four of em." He takes the bucket from my hand and carries it back to where the ingredients are stored. Again, he pours in the yeast, cornmeal, sugar, malted barley and hands me the stick. I mix as he dribbles in the water, and we repeat the process. When finished, he tells me to move the ladder to the second still and pour it in.

Once all four stills are filled with mash, Uncle

Jack grabs a couple pieces of wood and chucks it on the fire. "Now let's give her a little heat and we've got something going."

I follow suit and do the same with the other stills as Uncle Jack plops down on the straw bed and grabs his jar of moonshine. "Sit down here," he says as he points to a spot next to him. I walk over and take a seat, removing my hat as I wipe the sweat from my forehead. Not sure I like this hat anymore, I think. It's making me hotter. "Taste it," he says as he passes the jar to me. "If you're gonna brew it, you might as well know what it should taste like."

I hesitate for a moment before laying my hat on the straw next to me. I take the jar in both hands and lift it to my nose for a quick smell. The aroma is strong and pungent and I feel as if I can taste it already. I look at Uncle Jack, who is smiling as he watches me closely before I press the jar to my lips, tilt it to the sky and swallow. It burns from my mouth, down through my chest, and into my stomach. I cough and shake my head. It tastes awful and my eyes are watering. Why in the world would anyone drink this, I think to myself?

Uncle Jack slaps his leg and laughs uncontrollably. "Woo-hoo," He shouts loudly. "I remember my first drink. Bet my face looked just as sour as yours."

I pass the jar back to Uncle Jack. I can feel the moonshine burning in my stomach and feel a little lightheaded. Oh goodness, I think I'm drunk. I look to Uncle Jack for support, but he's having himself a shot and seems uninterested in my health.

I stand up and walk over to the stream that runs through the cave. I get down on all fours, stick my head down in the water, and gulp it up. I can still taste and smell it in my nostrils, so I do it again, but this time I take a bigger drink. Uncle Jack is laughing hysterically and keeps slapping himself on the leg. "Come on," he mutters through his giggling. "You'll be OK."

He waves me back over and once again I sit down next to him. He puts his arm around me and continues smiling as he gives me instruction. "Each batch you make has to be tasted. You'll get used to it, but you have to swish it around in your mouth to make sure it's right before you swallow. You don't want to get poisoned, and you don't want to poison anyone."

He stood up and motions for me to follow. "See those caps on the still with the copper tubing attached to it?" He was pointing to the top of the stills, and I could see what he was pointing at, so I nodded yes. "Good, now what we do is boil the mash and the vapors escape through the top, run down those tubes and get turned back into liquid here at the condenser. When there's no more vapor, we add more mash to the slop, and we continue the process." He stops pointing and turns to me. "You understand?"

I nod yes, even though I don't quite understand any of it. I know that if I try to really focus on it, that I will eventually get it. This all seems interesting to me, and I can't dismiss the feeling of excitement that I have. What is with my newfound interest? Why do I care now and hadn't just a day ago?

After thirty minutes or so, Uncle Jack picks up his jug and fills it from the spout where the moonshine collects at the condenser. He takes a swig and wipes his lips. "Perfection," he mutters while passing it to me. "Gotta give it a taste."

I take the jug, but stare at him for a moment. I'm not ready for this again. I just got over the last drink and its memory still lingers.

"Go ahead," he says with a reassuring smile and a gentle nod. "You'll get used to it."

This time, I take a very small drink and, just like Uncle Jack told me to, I swish it around in my mouth. It is as if it is actual fire, but somehow, I manage to swallow. Again, it leaves a burning trail as it makes its way down my insides to my stomach. I cough violently as I cover my mouth with both hands, feeling as if I am going to vomit it right back up.

Uncle Jack, for the second time, finds joy in my discomfort and lets out another laugh. "You'll get better," he says as he takes the jug from my hand and has himself another sip. "It's good so we can start filling the jars, just like yesterday."

I feel sick to my stomach, but I shake it off and I take my place as I had done the previous day and proceed to fill jars. I fill jar after jar and eventually the flow starts to die down. Uncle Jack has been monitoring my progress and notices the increase in time it takes to fill a jar.

"Come on," he says, while motioning for me to join him. "It's time to add more mash."

We repeat the process just like the first time around. Mix the mash, pour it into each still, wait for the moonshine to flow before filling more jars. Throughout the day, we repeat this process six or seven times and by the end of it; I am filling the stills and never lose flow, which Uncle Jack loves. He's watching and trying to teach me everything he knows. I think he loves both the company and the free labor. He sings and drinks and drinks and sings. Every so often, Sean would come in and have a drink with him before loading up cases and taking them back to the house to store in the shed. Each time, he's asking Uncle Jack how I'm doing and Uncle Jack's response each time is, "the kid is a natural."

The process is slow, and I have plenty of time to think. Today has been one of the biggest in my life and my emotions have been all over the place. From anger at the meeting with Dutch and Bobby to falling in love with the girl from the hotel. I fought with my brother and now embrace the life of a moonshiner and thirst for more. I want to see the girl from the hotel. If she is really Bobby's daughter, I can probably find her at the Kelley's house. Everyone in town knows Dutch has a big house in Murphysburg, a well-to-do neighborhood in Joplin and not too far from the hotel. Maybe she will be there, I think. I'll at least check it out and see.

Sean comes back into the cave one last time as we're pouring water over the fire. "All done?" he asks. "We need to take twenty cases down for Dutch. I'll take them by tomorrow."

Uncle Jack joins him at the door, and they share a shot of moonshine. "Any word from Patrick?" he asks.

Sean nods while taking another drink before wiping his mouth. "Yeah," he says. "They dropped supplies off in the shed and took off for Kansas City. Patrick is really excited about getting other customers."

Uncle Jack nods but doesn't smile. "He needs to be careful with Dutch," he replies. "That man is dangerous and shouldn't be fooled with."

Sean smiles a sheepish grin as he walks toward the finished product. "Yeah, he sure is."

I begin to get excited and hurry as I load the cart.

I know it'll only hold a few cases at a time, so I'll have to make multiple trips. I want to make it into town tonight; I must see her again. It'll take me an hour to get to Dutch's house. That's even if I left from here and cut through the woods.

"Slow down," Uncle Jack says as I fly past him. "You're gonna break the jars."

I don't stop. I'm running as I push the cart all the way through the cavern. When I get through the opening, I hope to see the rails complete and would be able to unload this stuff in a hurry, but Sean hasn't finished it. I grab the cases and hurry down to the car. There were still a few hours of daylight, and I wanted to see her again tonight.

I made my trip to the car and back up by the time Uncle Jack and Sean appeared from the mouth of the cavern. Uncle Jack is not nearly as drunk as last night, so he can help as the three of us load all the moonshine into the back of the car.

Uncle Jack climbs in the car and leans back as he is clearly exhausted. "I'll let you lads close it down," he says through heavy breathing. "I'll be right here waiting for you."

Determined to get on the road quickly, I take off up the hill and pass Sean near the opening of the cavern.

"Whoa, what's the hurry?" He asks.

I don't stop. I run down the cavern and into the cave, looking for more moonshine. Over in the corner are two cases, so I load them in the cart and take off toward the car.

Leaving Sean behind to extinguish the lanterns, I hear his voice echo off the walls as I exit, "You better not break anything and be home in time for dinner."

Chapter 5

Speechless

I make my way through the woods and eventually step out onto the sidewalk. The streetlights are already flickering, and I know it will be dark soon. I pick up my pace. I have to hurry if I want to catch any glimpse of the girl from my dreams. I had been lost in my thoughts during my travel to town, daydreaming of the possibilities. I imagined us falling hopelessly in love at the mere sight of one another, no conversation needed. However, the farther I travel, I realize that this is a childish dream as reality takes over and I second guess my decision to come and see her. She is normal, I worry, and needs to be courted. Her desires are the same as any girl her age and probably desires a man that can sweep her off her feet. I know I am not prepared for this, yet I continue forward, clutching to my delusion. My desire to see her overcomes my fear of contact. My heart races and my body releases gallons of sweat. I can feel the anxiety welling inside my body and I know it is useless to go to her house. She won't like you, I think, and she's too pretty for you. I weigh the consequences of my actions and agree that I have come too far for nothing. At the very least, I will wait around and not lay eyes on her. Anything above that is just a bonus.

I stop in my tracks and realize that I am standing in the middle of Murphysburg. I look around, searching through my memory and trying my best to remember how to get to Dutch's house. I had been there many times with my father as a child and yet, I can't remember. I close my eyes for a moment; it's a big white house. I can see it. I keep my eyes closed and continue to think about it. Two white lions out front. I have it; Dutch's house has two giant stone lions at the driveway entrance. That's what I'll search for.

I open my eyes and look around again. Murphysburg is not very big, maybe four or five square blocks, I believe. There aren't too many rich people in Joplin, so that limits my search. I turn and head north, keeping to the sidewalk and trying to stay out of the illumination of the street lamps. If someone sees me, Captain Lewis will surely take me to jail and it'll be easy to spot me this time of the day, as no one is out. I am the only one walking on the sidewalk and haven't seen anyone outside in any of the yards.

After only a block, I look to my left and spot the statues I search. Dutch's house is huge, the biggest in town and is surrounded by a large yard with a stone fence standing six feet high and running the entire length of the block, broken only by two large steel gates at the driveway entrance. They are closed and surely locked; I think. Probably not a good spot to enter. I cross the street and continue north along the wall. There are tall light posts mounted in the yard and illuminate the inside wall, which, to my benefit, cast shadows on the outside. I hang close to the wall, edging forward in the shadows. After travelling half the block, I come to an alley and the stone wall turns west, running the length of the block, separating the alley from the Kelley's property. I follow the wall and find the alley to be just as bright as the street side. I continue to walk close to the wall and search for a place to climb over. My heart is racing, and I feel exhilarated. My bold behavior is driven from some place deep within and I am a prisoner to my own actions.

Halfway down the block, I spot a guest house sitting about five feet from the wall and the light attached to the backside is burnt out. This is my access point, I feel as I peek around to see if anyone is around. I raise my arms to the top and grab a hold. My grip is loose, but I manage to pull myself high enough to sling my leg over. I drop to the ground directly behind the guest house. It's dark, no lights are shining while I quiet myself for a moment. I can almost hear my heart pounding in my chest, and I struggle to slow it down. I'm listening for dogs. I figure the Kelleys' must have guard dogs somewhere and I want to make sure they don't surprise me. Surely, they would have heard the noise I made as I dropped from the wall to the ground. Nothing, only the sound of my breathing, can be heard. I move over to the guest house and lift my head to peek in the window. It's dark and I am unable to see through. I turn, squat and lean my back against the wall of the guest house. What am I doing? Is all of this worth it? What do I hope to accomplish? I reason with myself and almost climb back over the wall, but my body will not listen to my mind. No. I have come this far, and I must see her again.

I move around the west side of the house, with each step being slow and cautious, watching and listening for any sound indicating people or dogs. I know they must be around somewhere. I reach the corner of the guest house and catch a glimpse of the Kelley's house. Every light must be on as a dim glow shines through each window and I search for her silhouette, but cannot find one. A brick sidewalk leads from the door of the guesthouse toward a patio attached to the back of the Kelley's house. It is cluttered with tables and chairs, allowing room for twenty people to gather, at least. To the left of the patio is an open yard and offers no cover. To the right, running the length and surrounding the patio, is a huge rose garden. Thick bushes mark the border surrounding it, and I dart in its direction. I jump into the bushes and land flat on my belly, directly on top of a rosebush. It hurts dearly, and I wince in pain as I roll off. I lay there feeling my stomach and search for the gaping hole it must have torn. I find only a scratch and rub it, trying to absolve the pain. I am covered in rose petals and surely my clothes are full of thorns, but my skin is intact, and my shirt has not been torn. I lay on my back for a moment, catching my breath and allowing the pain to disappear when all of a sudden, the porch light flickers on and the back door opens.

I roll to my left and press my body against the wall of bushes, trying to shield myself from the glow of the light. Someone must have seen me, maybe heard me as I landed on the rosebush, I worry. Why have I come here? Now I am certain that I will be sent to jail, left for days, and possibly forgotten. My breathing is heavy, and I strain to control it. The harder I try, the louder it gets. I hear footsteps, soft at first but growing louder as they approach. I have to run; I think. If I make it back to the wall, I have a good chance of escaping.

"Nice night out."

The voice is coming from the other side of the bushes and I peek around, positive they are speaking to me.

"Yeah, too nice to sit inside."

It's a second voice. They are talking to one another. Maybe I am safe.

"Got a light?"

I peek through the rose garden and see two silhouettes cast in the light from the porch. They are standing near me, facing one another. I hear the match strike and watch the shadow as one lights their cigarette and offers it to the other. One of them is much larger than the other, taller by almost a foot. I watched their shadow as they lift their cigarettes to their lips, inhale and rest their arm back at their side. I can feel my heart pounding through my ears. It's only a matter of time, I worry, before they find me hiding in the bushes.

"My dad is losing his edge."

The voice is familiar to me, and I recognize it as Bobby Kelley's.

"Why do you say that?"

The second voice is deeper than Bobby's, and I don't recognize it at all. It's not Dutch's, for sure. Bobby would not be talking to his father like this and it's not William Kelley, he would be hunched over, and his accent is too thick and I would notice. Who is it?

"He's getting soft. I would have killed the O'Connors' for betraying me and he let them walk away. Plus, he gave them more money."

I picture Bobby's face in my mind, probably scowling with his beady little eyes. Lips puckering under his mustache.

"Yeah, I was going to pull out my pistol when Patrick got loud." The unknown man says with a snicker. "But your dad shook his head no."

I know in that instant that it has to be Evan Blake, since he was the only other person at the meeting this morning.

"He had a real soft spot for their father, Mac." Bobby replies. "Loved him."

"That was before my time, huh?" asks Evan.

Bobby stays quiet for a moment. I watch his silhouette as he puffs on his cigarette, and I find it hard to believe that I'm lying here listening to them talk about my dad and my brother.

"Couldn't believe that boy was there today," Bobby says quietly without responding to Evan's question. "That brought up old memories."

Bobby and Evan are quiet again and remain that way for a while. The silence is almost unbearable as I struggle to lie perfectly still and silent. My feet are tangled in some barbs from the rosebush, and I want nothing more than to kick them loose. I had almost done it out of reflex a couple of times and had to catch myself.

"Couldn't believe that boy was there today," Bobby says again, repeating himself.

"Do you know him?" asks Evan.

Bobby chuckles aloud. "Do I know him? Yeah, I guess you could say that."

"What's so funny?" asks Evan. "Did I miss something?"

Bobby chuckles again. "You know that boy hasn't spoken in four years since the accident?" He pauses for another moment before repeating. "I can't believe he was there today."

Bobby's voice has gotten softer, and he speaks in almost a whisper. I have to strain to hear him and my body is frozen as I listen to him talk about me.

"Thought he was dead, too."

I am spellbound. What did he say? I tilt my head to get a better listen.

Evan flicks his cigarette in the bushes next to my feet. "Who was dead?"

"Shhhh." Bobby says as he also flicks his cigarette and grabs Evan by the arm. "I'll tell you, but you have to be quiet."

"I won't say anything. What is it?" Evan asks as his interest perks up.

Bobby steps back from Evan and takes a deep breath. "I killed their parents."

My heart stops beating. Did he say what I think he said?

"Went over there one night to pick up Mac. We had some things to tend to. Mac wasn't there, just his wife and she said he took the kids somewhere and would be back soon, so I decided to wait around for him. You should have seen her. Talk about beautiful."

I can't believe what I'm hearing. I am frozen in time. My muscles don't work, and my mind is running in forty different directions as Bobby continues his story.

"I courted her when we were kids." He says, while shifting his weight from one foot to the other. "I loved her, but she chose Mac, and I guess I never got over that."

Bobby's voice trails off again and Evan remains quiet. I lay there motionless, listening and waiting, my heart about to leap out of my chest.

"We were sitting on the sofa, making small talk,

and I guess my emotions took over. I grabbed hold of her and kissed her. I thought she wanted it as much as I did, but she pushed me away and slapped my face. I tried to tell her I was sorry, but she wouldn't hear it and started screaming for me to get out and wouldn't stop screaming. I apologized over and over. She was ranting and raving, said she was going to tell Mac and that he would kill me."

Bobby takes out another cigarette and lights it up. After inhaling deeply, he continues. "I got mad, real mad. I grabbed hold of her neck and was shaking her. I didn't know what I was doing; it was like I was out of my body. She fought me, but I overpowered her and the next thing I knew, she was lifeless. I tried to feel for a pulse, but she was dead."

Tears well in my eyes, and I can feel the bile building in my throat. I lose all sense and envision my mother, so full of life, being choked to death by Bobby Kelley. My heart is breaking, and I forget where I am. I have no worries about them finding me. I only listen to Bobby talk as I lie there feeling lifeless and now unable to move.

"You killed her?" Evan asks, a little louder than he would like.

Bobby remains quiet for a moment as he puffs on his cigarette. "Yeah, a crime of passion, I guess you can say. I didn't know what I was doing, and I was sorry for it right after."

"Oh, wow!" Evan exclaims. "Then what?"

"I did what anyone would do. I moved her body to the bedroom and laid her on the bed. She looked so peaceful lying there, like she was asleep. She truly was a beautiful woman."

Bobby's voice changes. He appears to snap out of the trance and realizes he has an audience in Evan. He puffs on his cigarette, and I can sense a change in his demeanor. He is acting tougher, I think.

"I watched her for a minute, and then I hear a car pull up. My car was in the driveway and I knew he saw it. I ran toward the door and found a fire poker by the fireplace. I grabbed it and jumped to the side as he opened the door. As soon as I saw his head, I swung that poker with all my power and hit him. The pointed end hit him in the forehead and blood splattered everywhere. I don't think he saw me or even knew what happened. His body dropped and then I saw the boy, standing there in the doorway."

"What boy?" asks Evan, clearly hanging on Bobby's every word. "The one with Patrick?"

Bobby nods his head. "Yep. He was young and just standing there watching his dad laying on the floor with blood flowing from his head. When he looked up at me, I swung again and hit him in the head. Not as hard as with Mac, but he went down and I couldn't find a pulse."

I feel a throbbing over the left side of my face, just above my ear. I remember now. I can feel the spot where Bobby hit me with the fire poker, and I remember the sight of my father lying on the floor. I see him opening the door and just as suddenly, falling to the floor. I can even hear the bone cracking hit that put him there. It is sickening, and I choke back tears. My father's blood had been running in a pool and I was watching it. Then I see Bobby's face. Wide eyed and surprised before everything eventually went black.

"I drug them both inside. I panicked for a minute,

and then I drug Mac in the bedroom with his wife. I couldn't get him on the bed, though; he was too big, so I left him lying on the floor. I didn't know what else to do, so I set the house on fire and got the hell out of there."

It stays quiet for a minute as they both stand facing one another. "What happened? What did you do with the boy?" Evan finally asks, breaking the silence.

"I thought he was dead too, so I drug him into the living room. That's the last place I saw him." Bobby pauses for a bit before continuing. "I heard he made it out and was in a coma at the hospital. I was gonna go up there and finish him, but I couldn't get past his brother Sean. He stayed there the whole time."

My memory came back to me again. I remember coming to and smoke was all through the house; I remember going to my parents' room and seeing the fire. I saw my mom on the bed and my father on the floor and their bodies were on fire. I remember stumbling my way to the back door before falling off the back porch. After that, I just remember waking up in the hospital.

"I hadn't seen him until today. I heard he was stupid and couldn't even talk, so I decided to let him be. That was until today. Did you see the way he looked at me?"

Evan takes a deep breath and sighs loudly. "Wow. So that's why you were so crazy at the meeting today. Must have been hard on you, seeing that boy there. How does your dad feel about that?"

Bobby quickly replies in a sharp tone, "Dad don't know and he can never know. Like I said, he loved Mac."

"OK," Evan says as he nods in agreement. "What do you want to do with them?"

"Kill them all." Bobby says as he takes a final puff

off his cigarette before tossing it in the bushes. "By the time we're done, there won't be any O'Connors' left."

Minutes pass after the two of them disappear back into the house and yet I remain hidden, pinned against the bushes. I haven't moved since they went inside. My mind and body are frozen in time as I try to process what just occurred. My eyes are tear soaked as I lay there imagining the horror my mother must have felt. I remember everything now, especially the pain I felt after I came to and stumbled into my parents' room to find their bodies on fire. I wanted to help them, but the smoke was unbearable, and I struggled to make it outside before I collapsed. The link to Bobby's face as he hit me with the poker was clear, crystal clear. I can see his gritted teeth as he swung with all his might. I relive the events of that evening over and over as I lay there in the Kelley's yard, shielded inside the rose bushes. It is fate that brought me here; I think to myself as I wipe away my tears. Fate brought me here to murder Bobby Kelley.

I stand to my feet and take a moment to brush away the dirt and leaves from my clothing as I search the Kelley's home for a way to get inside. I am on fire. My fear of being discovered has disappeared and I now want only one thing: to kill Bobby Kelley. My stomach burns, but I feel my hands are steady and my thoughts are clear. Focusing on my task, I feel immediate regret for not bringing along my rifle and pistol since I only carry a small pocket knife that my father had given me as a child. It is rarely used and I only carry it only as a token of his memory. I have come here for love but found hate. I only wanted to lay eyes on the most beautiful girl in the world, and now I intend to murder her father.

I walk around the wall of roses and brazenly stand on the patio, unafraid and unwavering. Looking up, I see that every light in the house is still on and think to myself that a few of the rooms must be empty and will allow me entrance. Dismissing the thought of climbing the side of the house, I realize I am already walking toward the back door. Surprised by my lack of fear, I watch as my hand reaches for the doorknob. Turning gently, I push open the door as if I am entering my own house. Stepping through the threshold, I softly close the door behind me and realize I am standing in a brightly lit kitchen. Without a second of hesitation, I sidestep into a darkened cupboard. Pressing my back against the wall, I close my eyes and listen to the sounds of the house. I can hear the slight buzzing of conversation and recognize the clinking and clanging of dishes. The sound is faint, but I can distinguish between five or six separate people, all located in the same place. Perfect, I think, it's dinner time and hope all the Kelley's are together, in one location.

I feel around in my pocket, finding my knife and pull it out. Covering it with the palm of my hand, I click it open and grip tightly. Momentarily hesitant, I step out into the lighted kitchen and gingerly walk into the open. The kitchen is empty, and I marvel at its size; big enough for a restaurant, I believe. The sound of the Kelley's dining is slightly louder and I know they must be in the next room. Unshaken, I find a stairwell to the right and move in that direction. The stairwell is narrow, and a light can be seen from the top, casting a shadow all the way down to the bottom, where I now stand. Beneath me, the stairs are carpeted red and lightly creak as I climb to the top.

Atop the staircase, I find a dimly lit corridor running the length of the house and lined with rooms on each side, similar to a hotel, I think. The first room on the left is a darkened washroom and directly across the hall from that is a closed door. I carefully walk up and press my ear to the door, listening for any sound of an occupant. When certain there is no one inside, I go in, closing the door behind me. The room is dark, lit only by the street lamp outside the window. I walk around the room and examine its contents. It is nicely decorated, but the dresser drawers are empty, and I find nothing hung in the closet. Must be a guest room, I think, and head back toward the door. Again, I press my ear to the door and listen for movement. Still nothing, so I open the door and poke my head out, glancing in both directions to ensure the coast is clear. I step back into the corridor and turn right, heading away from the staircase, and find another room on the left. The door is open and the light floods into the corridor. I hesitate for a moment before leaning beyond the door to gaze inside. The room appears empty, so I step in and look around. Unlike the room before, it is heavily decorated with trinkets cluttering the bureau and nightstand next to the bed. On the wall, above the bed, hang an arrangement of portraits and I step closer for a better look.

Immediately, I recognize the image of the girl from the hotel and feel my heart dance in my chest. I glance around the room and find a distinctive silver hairbrush lying on the nightstand next to the bed. While examining, I pick it up and pluck out a few of the auburn strands and let them fall to the floor. I immediately imagine her sitting on the corner of the bed, brushing her hair as she readied herself for sleep. I roll it over in my hand, finding an inscription on the back, "To my Emma." As I read it, I smile and think to myself how perfect the name fits as I repeat it in my mind over and over. Content with my finding, I place the brush back on the nightstand and again turn to the portraits hanging on the wall.

She really is beautiful, and the photos capture her essence and present her image in such a way that I find it hard not to get lost while staring at them. It doesn't take me long to pick out my favorite. She's sitting on a chair, her body turned slightly to the side amongst a backdrop of the rose garden I had been laying in just a few minutes earlier. Her hair is perfectly combed and positioned neatly over her shoulder. Her hands come together and rest on her knee. Her smile is breathtaking and gives pure life to the photo. I quickly pluck the portrait off the wall, remove the back of the frame, and pull the portrait out. I lift it to my eyes and give it a last look before folding it neatly and placing it in my pocket. I realize I am smiling as I stash the empty frame under the bed and move back toward the door.

Once I make it to the door, I take a moment to erase the thoughts of her and try to focus on my task of searching out Bobby Kelley. Directly across the hall is another room with the light shining into the hall. When I am certain no one is around, I quickly cross the hall and slip into the room. Again, this room is elegantly decorated, even more so than Emma's. It is larger too, complete with a sofa and chair and even has its own washroom. I walk around, inspecting the contents and again find portraits on the wall over the bed. Emma graces many of the images, as does her father Bobby and a woman, who I assume to be her mother. My heart fills with hate as I stare into Bobby's eyes, and I once again go back to the night he killed my parents. I can feel my demeanor change as evil takes over and I relive the pain that he caused my family. I have him; I think to myself while smiling despite my feelings. I will kill Bobby Kelley and redemption will be mine. I turn from the portraits and gaze around the room, looking for a hiding place that will allow me the same surprise attack that he was given when he jumped out and hit my father.

Out of nowhere, a hand brushes my shoulder. "Who are you?"

Immediately startled, I jump and spin around, sinking my knife to the handle in soft tissue and I feel a body go limp and crumple to the floor. I look down and recognize the beautiful face of none other than Emma Kelley.

Chapter 6

The Escape

Emma's expression is that of both surprise and anguish as she lay on the floor writhing in pain. One hand clutches her stomach with the other raised toward me, palm out, begging for mercy. Blood is seeping around her hand as she gasps for air through pitiful moans.

Instantly, I kneel by her side and put my hand over hers while she tries to push me away. I had not intended to hurt her. She is the reason for me being here and I want only to help her now as I feel guilt and despair about what has happened.

She is moaning and quietly calling for help. Without hesitation, I slip one arm around her neck and the other under her knees. I groan as I lift her and stumble toward the door. I am moving quickly yet her weight is heavy, and I clumsily hit her head on the door frame as I exit the room.

The thud only slightly delays my step as I make my way down the corridor toward the stairs. Moving quickly, I glance down and realize that I have knocked her unconscious. I labor with her body weight as I make my way down one step at a time and struggle to maintain my grip and my feet underneath me. My mind is racing as I have not thought this through and only now search for escape.

At the bottom of the stairs, I stop and listen for the sound of people in the kitchen. Emma's body lies lifeless in my arms, and her breathing is shallow. I hear only the clanking of dishes and the gentle hum of conversation a room over. I shift her weight to get a better grip and step out into the kitchen and head straight toward the door. Once there, I can barely grab the knob and turn, having to lift Emma's legs to complete the maneuver. Leaving the door open behind me, I cross the patio toward the back of the house and disappear out of the light, into the darkness.

I have no idea where I'm going. My heart is pounding, and my arms burn as I search the property for escape. In the opposite corner, forty yards away, I notice a stable surrounded by fencing and change direction. At the fence, I fall to my knees and lay Emma in the grass. Her lifeless body slumps out of my arms and rolls to the ground. I gasp for air and sit down while leaning my back against the wood of the fence. For the first time in a while, I feel a sense of calm spread over my body, and I glance over toward Emma. Her auburn hair partially covers her face, so I push her hair to the side and gently caress her cheek. She is so beautiful, and I feel a sense of sadness wash over me for what I have done. I lift her shirt to inspect the wound. Her stomach is smeared with blood and has pooled in her belly button. I take off my shirt and wipe away the excess blood, which exposes a small slit in her stomach that continues to seep blood. I wrap my shirt around her small body and tie it in place with a loose knot that I know won't hold if moved. I caress her cheek a second time, hoping to make her feel comfortable and stand to my feet.

The calm that I felt a moment earlier has

disappeared and is now replaced with anxiety. I must get out of here, and quickly I feel. I glance at the stable door and realize my feet are already moving in that direction. As I open the door, I begin to regret coming here. What drove me? What did I expect? Surely not this. I hadn't expected to hear what Bobby had done, and I certainly didn't want to hurt Emma. I pause for a moment as I think about the night Bobby had killed my parents. Anger rushes over me as I consider once again returning to the house and facing Bobby Kelley. I quickly dismiss the idea as I need to escape and get Emma to someone that can help.

My thoughts are interrupted as I reach the first stall. The sound of heavy breathing and hoof clattering cuts through the silence. Amongst the dim moonlight, I recognize the silhouette of the largest horse I have ever seen. As I turn to face it, the horse takes a few steps back and begins prancing in place. It is snorting and shaking its head up and down repeatedly. I reach my hand forward over the stall door and hold it steady while I quietly make shushing noises with my mouth. The horse continues snorting and prancing as it inches toward my hand. At first, it sticks its nose to my palm, breathing heavily, and I can feel the heat of its breath as it continues to snort and blow. I slowly move my hand upward, along its muzzle until I feel the crown of its skull. The horse has now slowed its head movement and begins a slight chuffing, allowing me to believe it is comfortable with me. As I rub the horse's forehead, I slowly move my free hand down the door and slide the bolt to open. As a familiar sound to the animal, the horse steps backward and prances in place before once again continuing to snort and shake its head. I cautiously open the door and step inside the threshold, again raising my hand toward the horse's head. Without hesitation, the horse stops prancing and moves forward to place its head on my hand. Almost immediately, the animal slows its movement and only chuffs lightly, indicating that it is comfortable with my presence.

Having been raised in the bottoms, I am familiar with horses going back as far as I can remember. Being poor, most folks, including my family, still use horses for transportation from time to time. They are used to pick up goods from the general store, daily travel back and forth to the mines, and even for a short ride to a neighbor's house for a visit. On weekends, most of the men from the bottoms get together for horse racing, where Crow is a frequent winner. He's the one who has taught me the most about horses and how to handle them. Sure, my father got me started and showed me plenty, but Crow was the one who worked with me and taught me how to handle myself and to be comfortable around them. It was only recently that Patrick sold our horses. Said he was tired of Sean and Ryan losing their money at the races and we had enough money for a couple of cars and a truck. Since there are roads leading thru the bottoms and up into the hills, we no longer need the horses. I wasn't upset about it as I got tired of taking care of the animals and I am always able to go to Crow's house and ride if I want to.

I continue rubbing the horse's head and slowly move around to its side while taking my other hand and rubbing down its back and side. It is now standing steady, and its breathing has slowed to a calm in and out. I glance to my right and find a bridle hanging from a nail on the wall. Still rubbing the forehead, I use my other hand to retrieve the bridle off the wall and step back around in front to face the animal. The horse's head snaps back quickly and lets out a neigh, but stays in place. "Shhhh", I sound lightly as I move my hand slowly up and down the entire length of the horse's muzzle, coaxing it to lower its head. As the horse brings its head down. I gently lift the bridle and slide the bit into its mouth, extending all the way to the corners. I reach up and push its ear forward under the headpiece, smooth out the straps, and fasten the buckle under its chin. As soon as I finish, the horse takes a step forward, seeming to know that we are leaving the stable. I grip the reins firmly and turn while walking the animal out of the stall and toward the door. There is no hesitation from either of us as we step out of the stable and into the moonlight. Immediately, I notice a slight movement from Emma as I lead the horse to where she is laying.

She is slowly moving each foot back and forth, rocking them ever so gently as she writhes in pain. Both of her hands have moved down to cover her stomach, and she is quietly moaning. I wrap the reins over the fence railing and kneel by her side. As I place my hand on hers, she opens her eyes, and she gasps as she tries to call for help. "Shhh", I softly whisper as I move her hands away to get a better a better look at the bandage.

"Stop, leave me alone", she mumbles through shortened breaths.

As I move both of her hands to the side, I can feel her weakly pressing back against mine. I glance at the bandage and notice blood has seeped thru the shirt in a few spots. It is good that it is not pouring blood, but I know I need to apply pressure on it if I have any hope of stopping it completely, as I know she can't afford to lose much blood. I take her right hand and cover the wound on her stomach and place my hand on top of hers, pushing down gently to apply pressure. I turn to face her and notice she is staring at me with tears streaming from the corners of her eyes.

"Why?" she mutters softly while staring deeply into my eyes.

I don't answer. I just hold my hand over hers and stare back into her eyes for a moment in hopes she will understand that I have no intention of hurting her any further. We sit there looking at each other for only a few moments before lights flash across my eyes. A car turns down the street and is driving directly toward the gate next to the stables. I lay down next to Emma and pull her lower body back into the shadows next to mine. I can hear the engine get louder as it grows nearer and I lift my head slightly, only to catch a glimpse as the car turns left and continues up the street. This brings me back inside the situation and I know I have to get moving or risk getting caught. There has been enough time to pass that someone would come looking for her soon, I believe. I get back to my knees and look around. No movement anywhere and the same lights still shine from the house as before.

I move Emma's arms up around my neck and she moves them back down, pushing on me with all the strength she can muster. I lean her up into a sitting position and put both of my arms under her armpits while locking my hands together. I use all my power to stand up. My knees are shaking, and I wince as Emma buries her fingernails in the bare skin of my back and digs in deeply.

"Stop it, let me go!" She says thru gritted teeth.

She is fighting back stronger now, but it is not enough as I eventually get her to her feet and carry her the short way to where I have the horse tied. Once we arrive at the horse, I lean her back against its forelimbs. She is still scratching me and begs me to stop, but she can barely stand on her own two feet. I turn her body facing the horse and, while using the animal's forelimbs as a brace; I reach down and wrap my arms around both of her knees. The horse is calm and stays in place as I lift Emma upwards. She groans loudly as her body slides against the body of the horse. It is tall, so I hold Emma's knees with one arm while reaching down to grab her feet with the other. One of her feet is missing a shoe, so I grab onto the bottom of the one with a shoe and push with all my strength as her body crests the top of the horses back and comes to rest with her stomach directly where its neck meets its back. I duck under the neck of the horse and walk around to the other side. Emma has gone limp through the process and her arms are dangling down the side of the horse. I pick her head up and can see her tear soaked eyelids are closed as she has passed out, most likely from the pain of her wound being drug across a horse's back and from being weak with the loss of blood.

The horse is breathing heavier now and gently lifting its leg before placing it back on the ground over and over. I can see its eye is gazing back at me and following my movement as I walk to the fence and unwrap the reins. I turn the horse toward the gate and walk to the edge of the shadows. I stop for a moment, looking in all directions for movement but see nothing. I hold my breath and listen to the darkness for any sign of people. Nothing, I think. I step out into the moonlight and quickly lead the horse to the gate. Without hesitation, the horse follows as I open the gate and walk out into the street. To my left, I notice a tree stump and lead the horse directly in front of it. I lift the reins over the horse's back, climb on the tree stump, grab a handful of hair before jumping on the horse's back, all while pulling myself upright with my legs. I scoot forward toward Emma and pull her back to my knees as I steady her for a ride. I reach under her stomach and feel the dampness of blood across my fingers. The makeshift bandage had slid while getting her on the horse and currently sits untied. I gently tuck the shirt under her stomach, creating a barrier between her wound and horse's back. I maneuver her body to apply pressure to the wound before grabbing the reins and preparing to ride.

While sitting atop the horse in the glow of the streetlight, I finally notice that it is a beautiful black thoroughbred male. Its coat glistens in the light and mane flows beautifully, indicating this horse is valuable and probably well taken care of. Most likely a racehorse worth a lot of money, I believe. I grab the reins and gently tap the horse with my heels and head toward the alleyway. The night is quiet and I am positive the sound of the hooves can be heard, which might alert someone to investigate. It will not be good if someone catches me on a stolen horse carrying an unconscious girl with a stab wound. Once we reach the alley, I tap my heels again and the horse begins to trot. Emma's lifeless body is bouncing slightly with each step, so I press my open hand against her back to keep her steady. When we reach the end of the alley, I turn left and keep moving at a steady pace. I need to get off the streets and soon.

As we ride, I frantically search for a familiar

landmark that will give me some sign as to where I am. All the while, I am looking to make sure no one has spotted us and gives chase. I'm not quite sure, as we are moving at a pretty good pace, but that is the least of my concern. The farther we travel, the more frazzled I become. I know I can't go down main street as it is too busy and I'm sure to be caught. That is the only way I know to get me home, and it worries me not being able to go that way.

While taking a right turn, my body slides and I have to grip my legs around the body of the horse to keep from falling off. The muscles in my legs already burn and I have a pain in my bottom from not having a saddle. This is the first time I've ever ridden without a saddle and I already know I don't want to do it again. As my attention is focused on keeping Emma and me on top of the horse, I recognize the city park just ahead of our current direction. My parents used to take us to this park for picnics and to play. I know there are railroad tracks leading from the park to Turkey Creek bridge and I can get home from there.

"Hey, are you OK?"

The sound cuts through my thoughts like a bullet. I don't look back, I just heel the horse and take off as quickly as possible. As we cross the street into the park, there is a slight incline, and as the horse climbs up, Emma and I slide to the back. We would have fallen off, but just as we got to the tail, the horse crests the hill and flings our momentum forward. I don't stop or slow down. As we ride toward the tree line, I use my legs and knees to scoot Emma and me closer to the horse's head and the center of its body. She still has not woken and I am getting worried about her. I am also concerned the man I heard yell out is coming for us, but my main focus is to get Emma to help. We are moving fast and the bright moonlight illuminates obstacles, allowing for plenty of time to maneuver around them.

About 30 yards before we reach the tree line, I pull back on the reins to slow us down. The horse slows quickly and lurches our bodies forward. I recover quickly and position our bodies back to where we are comfortable as I turn the horse left and walk us down the tree line. I search frantically for the train tracks as we inevitably reach the end of the park. Both sides of this corner show nothing but trees, and I cannot find an opening to the tracks.

I pull back on the reins, bringing us to a dead stop. I look left and see nothing. I turn the horse around, back toward the direction we just rode from, and see it off in the distance. All the way at the other end of the park, I see our town's small depot. Without hesitation, I heel the horse and take off in that direction, traveling back the exact way we had come. As we ride past the point that I had turned off, I again heard a voice sound out from the darkness.

The person yelling at me is off in the distance and I'm unable to make out what they are saying. I don't slow down or look in their direction. I heel the horse again and pick up speed. Emma's body is bouncing dangerously heavy, so I take one hand off the reins and scoot her body back just slightly over my knees and up toward my stomach. I then place my hand around her body and hold pressure on her body against mine. The sound of the horse's heavy breathing combined with the sharp, hollow sound of his hoofs striking the ground is exhilarating. Gone is my fear, and I am fixed in the moment. My heart races and my palms are sweaty. I grip the reins tighter and pull back lightly as we near the depot. Without an ounce of hesitation, I turn us left and then right to navigate around the depot deck. With a slight upward jump, we are over the gravel and up onto the tracks. I immediately pull the reins back and to the left, leading the horse perfectly. We are in sync as if we are one as we continue down the tracks. Within moments, trees consume us on both sides and the lights grow dim behind us.

After a few minutes, I pull the reins back to a stop. I listen beyond the horse's heavy breathing, through the chirping and buzzing of insects in the night, listening for any sign we are being followed. I look back and can't see anyone, nor do I hear them. I extend my hand down to Emma's face and push her hair back. I run my fingers along her face and feel the warmth of her cheeks as I position my finger under her nose. Her breathing is shallow and slow, but steady. I bring my hand up under her stomach and feel the dampness of blood again. I take a moment to reposition the makeshift bandage before tapping my heels on the horse's belly to continue our journey.

As we make our way down the tracks, I keep the horse at a steady walk. I frequently glance behind us to ensure no one is following. I know I need to get home as fast as I can. I just don't want to risk the horse stumbling or accidentally drop Emma. I shiver as a gust of wind brushes across my shirtless body. I can now feel the stinging pain in my back where Emma had scratched me. I feel alone and scared. What have I done? I traveled all that way just to catch a glimpse of a girl I don't even know and now I carry her lifeless body with me down the railroad tracks on a stolen horse no less. A sense of sadness washes over me as a tear falls from my eye and rolls down my cheek. Nothing will be the same as I have now murdered someone, I worry. Not just anyone, but a sweet, innocent young girl that hurt no one or anything. I think back to the hotel and visualize her smiling face as she bounds the hallway. So happy. So pretty. She doesn't know me, yet I come into her home and stab her. Why didn't I leave her, I wonder? Why did I kidnap her and where am I going? I can't take her to my house. Patrick is in Kansas City and I know Sean won't be home for hours. I can't take her to a doctor and know I can't just take her back to her home. They will surely kill me. Then it hits me. I can take her to Crow's house. He's good with medicine. Maybe he can help her and will tell me what to do next. That's it, I agree, I can always count on Crow.

With a newly found sense of direction, I heel the horse and pick up speed. We're not far and I want to get there as quickly as possible. It can't be good for her to be slumped over the horse like this and probably hurting her. What about her mother, I wonder? Surely, they have discovered her missing, and her mother must be worried sick. For a moment, I feel sorry for her family as I think about her mother missing her child. But just as quickly as the feeling came, it leaves as I picture her father's face. For the first time since this ordeal began, I remember his words and picture his evil. I relive the moment, relive the horror of him killing my mother and father. I see his face as he hit me with the poker. I can feel it in my mind. I am boiling with anger, and I want revenge. Wait until I tell Patrick and Sean what he's done. He will regret doing this and we will kill him for it!

A raindrop falls from the sky and lands on my

hand, holding the reins. Another drop falls and within moments, I am in the middle of a full-on downpour. I slump slightly forward to shield Emma's body as much as possible. We are coming out of a bend in the tracks, and I can't see very well anymore. Not only is the rain hitting my eyes and running down my face, but it has gotten darker with the storm and my visibility is limited. I squint my eyes and recognize the Turkey Creek bridge shortly off in the distance.

I have seen this bridge almost daily since I was old enough to walk. I run these hills and know I can get to Crow's from here, even with my eyes closed, I believe. I slow the horse and pull the reins right. I grip onto Emma's body as we descend the tracks into a sloppy ditch that is moderately filled with water. Gripping tightly with my legs, I heel the horse, and he pulls us up out of the ditch with ease. Emma's body slides backward a little, but I am able to hold on and stabilize her as we level out on the road before trotting a few yards to the covered bridge where we come to a stop. I think about staying under here and out of the rain for a moment. I am sure the dirt has turned to mud and is bound to be slippery. Without another thought about it, I heel the horse and continue down the road. I am freezing as we make turn after turn, navigating the curvy roads through the hills. The horse is surefooted and moves steadily toward the bottoms as I clutch the reins and hold Emma close to my body.

After what seems like an eternity, I finally see the intermittent glow of lights ahead. We have reached the bottoms. I stop for a moment to think about what I should do. I need to get to Crow's house without being seen. Most people around here keep their nose out of other people's business, but I believe it to be better if they don't see me at all. In my head, I quickly map out the fastest route with the fewest houses and reason with myself that these people should be inside because of the rain. I heel the horse and continue, moving in a path that I believe to shield me from view. Navigating as I go, I make my way past our house and cut through the backyard, which is directly connected to Crow's yard. I ride the horse around the house, noticing there are many candles still lit and hoping he is awake. Just as I arrive at his front door, the door flies open and a shirtless Crow appears, pointing a rifle at my head.

I sit square up on the back of the horse, push my chest out, and lift my head up so he can see my face. And through a pitiful tone, I simply cry out, "Help!"

Chapter 7

The Consequence

Bewildered, Crow's head lurches back and his mouth falls open as soon as he recognizes me. He stands there staring at me for a moment before finally sitting his gun by the door. He descends the steps and is standing at my side with the quickness of a mountain lion after prey. He reaches up and pulls me from the mount, setting my feet on the ground and I can feel my legs cramping, and I take a moment to gain my footing.

"She's been stabbed", I proclaim as I stare directly into his eyes.

Crow nods but says nothing before reaching up and gingerly putting his hand under the lifeless body of Emma. He places his other hand on her legs and slides her off the back of the horse. As she slides, he moves his left arm under her legs and twists her body so that her back is now resting on his right forearm. The blood-soaked shirt I had used as a bandage falls needlessly to the ground and is stomped into the mud as Crow takes his first step toward the house. Again, and just as quickly as before, he is up the stairs and across the threshold before I have even turned toward the door. Gaining my composure, I tie the reins around the porch railing and shuffle inside.

"How long?" Crow asks as I close the door

behind me.

"About an hour," I respond while glancing down at Emma after he lays her on the floor.

Crow is already removing Emma's clothes. As he lifts her dress above her underpants, I can see the wound is open and still seeping blood. Her body is limp as he negotiates her arms through the holes. I turn my head in shame, unable to look at her. I am responsible for her death and cannot watch as he works to help her.

"Get some water and rags off the shelf," Crow calls out, cutting through my thoughts.

I walk into the kitchen and find a pitcher of water sitting on the counter. I pick up a bowl that sits nearby and empty the contents of the pitcher into the bowl, which fills to the top. I pick up the bowl of water with both hands and looked around for rags. With each step, I continually spill water on the floor and find it difficult to stabilize my hands. In the far corner, on a shelf and next to a bag of rice, I see a stack of rags. I walk to the shelf with disoriented thoughts and can't figure out how to pick up the rags with my hands full. I stop for a moment, take a deep breath and hesitate briefly before sitting the bowl back on the table. I retrieve the rags, stick them under my arm, and pick up the bowl a second time.

As I return to the living room, I continue to spill water with each step. I kneel beside Emma and place the water bowl on the floor before trying to hand the rags to Crow.

"Clean the wound while I get supplies," he says as he stands to his feet and exits the room.

Crow has wrapped Emma with one blanket around her upper body and another blanket covering her lower body. She is lying on a blanket on the floor and is propped up using large, brightly colored pillows. I dip one rag in the water and ring out the excess. Gingerly, I start at the furthermost point of the bloodstains and began wiping away. A lot of the blood has dried and was difficult to clear. I try to be cautious of the wound but need to scrub with what effort I believe is OK. Once I get to the opening of the wound, I retrieve a fresh cloth and dampen it before wringing it almost dry. I blot delicately and dab each droplet of blood as it protrudes from her flesh. As I scan her stomach area, I realize her body is still smeared with blood, so I hold a fresh rag over her wound to stop the bleeding while I continue cleaning the other areas.

"That'll work." Crow states as he reappears from the other room. He kneels beside her and moves my hands to the side while pouring whisky over the wound. He put the bottle down beside him but quickly picks it up again, takes a swallow himself before pouring another shot over the wound.

"This will help prevent infection and slow the fever," he says to me as he applies a generous amount of yellow paste to the stab wound. He then pulls out a bed sheet that he had laid behind him and takes out his knife. He cuts the bed sheet about six inches thick from the side and runs the entire length to the bottom. Crow applies gauze to the wounded area and leans Emma's body forward, gently wrapping the sheet around her midsection and pulling it as tight as he could without cutting off circulation. Once he finishes wrapping her body, he reaches his arm under her legs and picks her up before disappearing into the other room.

I remain seated, staring at the blood-soaked rags

in disbelief and thinking about how fragile Emma now appears to be. Something deep inside me wants her to be OK and I pray that she is. Not because I am afraid of getting in trouble, it is something else. I have feelings for her; I believe. Something similar to the way I feel about my family, maybe deeper. Do I love her?

"What happened to the girl?" Crow asks as he once again reappears in the doorway and walks toward me.

I glance up and lock eyes with him. I can feel tears welling in my eyes as a lump forms in my throat. "I saw her today, and I wanted to see her again."

Crow stops in front of me and stands there staring, closed mouth and tight-lipped as I continue. "I went to her house and then I stabbed her," I cry out despairingly. Tears spill down my cheeks and I don't bother to wipe them away.

He kneels beside me, placing a hand on my back, and calmly asks, "What do you mean you stabbed her?"

I turn toward him and fall back on my bottom. I wipe the tears away and stare directly into Crow's eyes. "I did this," I mumble. "I stabbed Emma Kelley on accident."

Crow's face, though already solemn, turns to stone. "What do you mean Emma Kelly?" he asks directly. "Is she related to Dutch?"

I turn my head and again peer at all the bloody rags before responding. "She is his granddaughter."

His hand fell from my back and Crow also drops to his bottom next to me. I look back up at his face and see the muscles in his jaw clenching and releasing over and over. We just sit there for a minute, staring into each other's eyes as he comes to fully realize the magnitude of the situation.

"I didn't mean to." I say to him while breaking the silence. "It was an accident."

I take a deep breath, hoping to control my emotions as I tell him the story of what had happened tonight, desperately trying not to leave out a single detail. I tell him how I hid in the bushes and overheard Bobby talking about killing my folks. I tell him about how I went in the house, intending to kill Bobby Kelley. I tell him how I escaped and what drove me to bring her to his house. Crow listens intently, never speaking but nodding his head from time to time. At some point, he has placed his hand back on my shoulder and runs it through my hair now and then, trying to show support. With a nod of his head and the tender caress of his hand, I feel at ease telling him what happened. At each part of the story, I feel a range of emotions across my entire body. From anger when discussing Bobby to remorse when discussing Emma. Crow must have felt the same as I witnessed his demeanor change with each setting and consequent outcome.

Once finished, we each sit in silence for a moment and stare at each other. Crow has now softened his jaw, and he appears to be searching for a resolution. "Did anyone see you come here?" He asks, nodding back toward the door.

I shake my head no, but also shrug my shoulders. "I don't think so, but I'm not sure," I respond. "It was very dark and raining heavily."

He takes a deep breath in through his nose while looking down at my trousers. "You must be cold and uncomfortable. You're soaked to the bone."

I look down and realize that I had forgotten how

wet I am. Almost immediately, my body recognizes that I am cold, and I begin to shiver.

"Go change your clothes." He says as he stands to his feet, once again regaining his composure. "I will figure out what to do here until Patrick gets home."

I immediately stand to my feet and nod my head in agreement. As I turn toward the door, I hear Crow mutter softly, "It's nice to hear you talk again." I don't stop or acknowledge his words. I simply continue forward out the door, only stopping for a moment on the porch to allow my eyes to adjust to the darkness outside. The rain has already reduced to a gentle sprinkle, enabling for better vision as I make my way from Crow's house to our back door.

Only a dim light is visible in the kitchen as I lightly turn the knob. The top of the door creates a slight scrape since it doesn't quite sit right in the frame. I step through and gently close the door behind me, not completely pulling it closed. I peer down at my new shoes and realize they are completely covered in mud. With no forethought, I use my left foot to remove my right shoe and then my right foot to remove my left shoe. As I bend down to pick up my shoes, I realize that this is an unconscious effort to prevent dirtying Sara's floor. Understanding this makes me smile as I quickly but quietly make my way across the kitchen, into the living room, and up the stairs. Many steps groan as I climb my way to the top. As I peak the staircase, I hesitate briefly and peer down the hall at Sara and Patrick's bedroom. She is not visible, nor are there any sounds indicating she's awake, so I turn and walk briskly down the hallway and into my bedroom. No Sean, anywhere and I feel as if I'm alone.

Once inside, I leave the door open as I hurry to the dresser. Watching for Sara, I glance over my shoulder and back toward the door, catching a glimpse of clothing stacked on my bed. Still holding my shoes in one hand, I turn and tiptoe to my bed. Folded neatly sit a stack of brand-new clothes similar to the ones Patrick had bought for me earlier. There are three sets of clothes, all in different colors. Quickly, I select a black pair of knickers, black socks, and a blue shirt from the pile. Turning on my heels, I tiptoe out of my bedroom and across the hall to the bathroom. The door is closed, so I gently put my shoes on the floor and twist the knob. The knob squeaks when turned and the door creaks while opening so I sling it open as quickly as I can. Without another thought, I grab my shoes, step inside, and close the door with my foot. While turning on the light, I catch a glimpse of myself in the mirror. My hair is soaking wet, face dirty, and blood streaks stain most my torso. I lay the shoes on the floor, the clothes on the counter, before collecting a washcloth from the cabinet. Turning on the faucet, I run my hand under the water a few times before finally sticking my head fully under the stream. I am cold already and the water sends chills throughout my entire body and feels as though my scalp is being stabbed with a thousand pins. I finish rinsing my hair and dampen the cloth before wiping my face, hands, arms, and chest. The blood had dried somewhat but was much easier to remove than that stuck on Emma's body. Once finished, I turn the water off and remove the last of my clothing.

After putting on my underpants, I sit down on the edge of the tub as I begin to feel exhaustion set in. Emotion consumes my thoughts. I am sad, angry, scared; all at once. And for a moment, I cry aloud. I am tired and want nothing more than to climb into my bed and erase this day from memory. But how can I? Look at how much I have gone through tonight. I hate Bobby Kelley; I think. A fire once again rises in my stomach and energizes me as if a bolt of lightning struck my heart. I quickly put one sock on, then the other, and stand to my feet. I want to kill Bobby. Not Patrick, or Sean, or Crow, but me. I want it to be me. I slip on my knickers, realizing they fit looser than before, and I decide I will need my suspenders. I quickly slide the shirt over my body and loosely tuck it into my trousers. Picking up my shoes, I decide to wipe off the mud and pick up the used washcloth. Sitting back down on the edge of the tub, I wipe the excess mud from around the sole. How will I do it, I wonder? I will go back tonight and kill him. I need my gun. As I clean my shoes, I witness the emotion leaving my body. I am no longer sad, nor angry. I am nothing at all. All emotions have now been replaced with a drive and desire to kill Bobby Kelly. It comes from deep within and is absolutely clear to me. My heart dances inside my chest and I feel as if it will burst as I know what I need to do.

I finish tying my shoes and dispose of the loose clumps of mud. After piling my dirty clothes in the tub, I open the door and come face to face with Sara as she stands just outside the door.

"Where have you been?" She asks with her arms crossed firmly in front of her.

Sara doesn't wait for an answer, nor does she expect one. She pushes past me and walks straight to the tub. While picking up my dirty clothes and washcloth, she gives me a look of disappointment. "Cieran, what happened to this wash cloth?" she asks.

I glance down nervously. She is holding my clothes under one arm and has the mud-stained wash cloth pinched with two fingers, holding it in the air. The blood stains have been replaced by layers of mud from cleaning my shoes. I breathe a sigh of relief and turn out the door, entering my room.

Sara follows and stands in the doorway as I fetch my suspenders and put them on.

"You look good," she says with a comforting smile and seeming to forget the mud-covered washcloth.

I turn to look at her while I finish buttoning my suspenders and puff out my chest. I give Sara a little smile, as I know how much she cares about me and how she constantly worries. If she ever knew what I did tonight, I think to myself, it will destroy her.

"I really wish you wouldn't go back out," she says in a somber tone. "It's getting pretty late, and the rain made it muddy. You better not ruin those clothes."

I look into her eyes and feel her love for me. She's not mad, nor is she getting onto me. She is just making conversation and attempting to be motherly. Sara is used to me being outside late at night. She knows I don't like to sit inside and that I usually run around the hills or mess around in the bottoms. It's fairly loose around the house, which I have to admit is a blessing tonight. All of us come and go as we please, only to be scolded by Patrick if we cross a line or get into trouble. Sean isn't even immune to Patrick's preaching sometimes.

As I walk toward the door, Sara steps back and turns to the side, allowing me to pass by easily. Once at her side, I pause for a moment and lean into her while wrapping both arms around her as I nestle in for a hug.

She immediately drops my clothing and smothers me with her arms. I've never hugged her before, and she takes full advantage of the opportunity. She pulls me in close and rubs my back while squeezing tightly. When I pull back, she lets go and slides one hand to my cheek, rubbing it with her thumb.

"You're a good boy," she says through trembling lips and appears as if she is going to cry.

I fake a smile and take a step back. Collecting herself, Sara bends down and retrieves the clothes from the floor. While trying to hide her emotions, she jokingly states, "As long as you don't ruin anymore wash cloths."

My smile opens even larger as I turn to walk down the stairs.

"What is this?" she asks, catching my attention.

I turn back around and see that Sara is fishing something out of my pocket. My heart sinks as I watch her pull my knife and photo of Emma out of the pocket of my dirty trousers. Before I realize what, I'm doing, I snatch the items from her hand while turning and running down the stairs into the kitchen.

"There's ham and cheese for a sandwich in the icebox." Sara yells at me as she makes her way downstairs. I half turn, give a nod, before walking out the back door.

Stepping into the night, I realize the rain has subsided and has been replaced with humid warmth. There's barely a breeze and at least ten degrees warmer, I feel. I walk directly to the shed and retrieve my pistol from its hiding spot. While sticking it in the band of my trousers, I figure they're too loose to hold the pistol firmly and settle for my pocket. It felt awkward since I wasn't used to carrying it. I don't like the way it feels in my pocket. I usually only carry my rifle, so I pick up my father's old leather satchel and wipe the dust away. He used to carry this satchel with him almost daily when he left the house for work. I wasn't sure what he carried in it, but I know that's where he kept his lunch that my mom would make for him most days. It was one of the few personal items left since everything burned up in the fire. Patrick had found it in his automobile a few days later and I snagged it the first chance I got. I slung the strap over my shoulder and opened the clasp. Grabbing boxes of bullets, I added them neatly in the bottom of the bag. Once I figure I have enough ammunition, I pull the pistol from my pocket and place it on top before also adding the photo of Emma and my pocketknife. I buckle the clasp, pick up my rifle and tuck it under my arm before turning and walking toward Crow's house.

As I step inside, Crow is busy stuffing blankets in a knapsack, and he barely acknowledges my presence. I follow as he walks to the kitchen and adds handfuls of food from his cupboard. He hands me the knapsack and disappears into the back of the house. After only a few moments, he reappears with a handful of gauze and a couple of small containers. Walking back over, he motions for me to open the knapsack and places the gauze inside. "This is an antibiotic," he states as he lifts the container for me to see. "This one is an old Indian medicine," he says while lifting the other. "Use both and make sure to wash out the wound with whisky when you change the dressing."

"Where will you be?" I ask, confused.

Crow put both jars in the knapsack before replying, "I'm taking you both to the hills and you can hide in the cave until Patrick gets back. He'll be back the day after tomorrow and he will know what to do. Hopefully, the girl don't die by then. We'll see if Sean knows any doctors that can help and won't say anything."

I stare at Crow quizzically. "What about Sara?" I ask.

"I don't know," he replies. "Maybe we'll tell her you're hunting."

I am still staring at Crow and think to myself that he looks oddly nervous. Crow is a tough, but calm man. I have never seen him get angry or lose his cool, even when he gets into fights at the horse races. He will usually stand his ground while calmly trying to diffuse the situation and never throws the first punch. But boy, let me tell you, he is tough to handle.

Without another word, Crow walks away, slipping into the next room. When he returns, he has Emma cradled in his arms and I can see he has dressed her while I was away. Emma is now wearing a pair of Crow's pants with the bottoms rolled up, exposing her bare feet and hang loosely around her legs and waist. He has tied a makeshift belt around her waist, but it is not drawn tight. The shirt is white and lays loosely over her torso. The neck has fallen to one side and exposes the top of her shoulder. She looks almost comical, I think, but I don't find it funny.

"Grab the blankets off the bed," Crow says, gesturing with his head in the direction I should take.

I walk into the bedroom and see the two blankets he had used earlier. With the knapsack in one hand, my father's satchel over my shoulder, and my rifle in the other, I stand there for a moment trying to figure out how I can carry it all. I put everything down on the floor and laid out the blankets. Then I put my rifle in the middle and rolled the blankets tightly around the gun. I tuck the bundle under my arm, sling the satchel back over my shoulder, and pick up the knapsack.

Crow is waiting for me as I enter the room and immediately turns and walks out the door without speaking. I pick up my pace, following him toward the stables. Instead of going inside, he turns and heads for the back of our property on foot, disappearing into the shadows. Crow is moving fast, and I have to almost trot to catch back up. We move cautiously through yards, staying in the shadows. When crossing the few roads we come upon, he always hesitates briefly while looking around before moving quickly across and always finding the shadows. Within minutes, we are past the bottoms and are making our way across the meadowlands. The grass is high and since it had rained, is difficult to walk through. Even while carrying Emma, Crow seems to find it much easier than I. He is stepping high and trampling through with almost no visible discomfort. I push forward, knowing it isn't very far between the meadowlands and the unchallenging trails leading through the hills.

We cut across the road. The moonlight illuminates our presence as we climb a small hill. Once at the top, trees rise into the sky as the hills are heavily wooded and roll for miles and miles while it gradually gets higher. Off slightly to the left, a dark hole breaks through the tree line, marking the entrance into the trails. As we step into the darkness, Crow stops, looks back at me for a moment, then continues forward. He is moving faster than before, and I am at almost a jog as I struggle to keep up. It takes a while before my eyes adjust completely to the dark, but it doesn't really matter. Both Crow and I know these trails like the back of our hand. I travel them almost daily and have no issues navigating in the dark. We move stealthily through, twisting and turning as they lead through the hills. Every so often, we turn off on a trail that leads in a different direction or climbs higher into the hills.

"How long have you been talking?" Crow asks; his voice cutting through the silence like a gunshot.

My breathing is heavy, and I wait a moment before answering. "Today," I respond.

Crow continues forward, not slowing a bit as he moves through the trails. The gun and blankets are uncomfortable, so I adjust my hold to get a better grip. I can feel the sweat from my palms soaking into the knapsack. I always had sweaty palms, I think to myself.

"I always could," I continue without prompting. "I guess I just didn't want to."

Crow laughs aloud. "I guess there should be more people like you," he replies.

I don't know what that means; I think to myself. I usually have a hard time understanding jokes. "Is she gonna die?" I ask.

"Not sure," he quickly replies. "It is a small knife wound, but she lost a lot of blood. We have to keep it clean and make sure she doesn't get an infection. A doctor can help, but I don't know any."

Crow slows down a little. "Why were you there tonight?" He asks.

I sling the knapsack over my shoulder to see if that will be more comfortable. It feels better; I think, so I leave it and begin to tell him the story about how I saw her at the meeting. How I thought she was beautiful and how I just wanted to see her again.

Crow laughs aloud again. "Women," he cries out. "That's what they do to you. Will make you walk miles just to look into their eyes."

"I didn't mean to hurt her." I reply, feeling the guilt once again wash over me. "I was going to kill Bobby Kelley, and she scared me." I once again picture her eyes as I stuck the knife in her belly. Those beautiful green eyes grew large, and terror shined through. "I'm gonna kill him still."

Crow stopped dead in his tracks and turns back to face me. He reaches out with his left hand under Emma's legs and grabs my arm. "Don't do anything until Patrick gets back." He says while stone faced. "Promise me you won't go back."

He is stern and stares at me intently. I am dead set on returning to get my revenge, but I am also scared. I know they will look for Emma and will most likely have hired guns everywhere. It will be almost impossible for me to get to Bobby. It will be a suicide mission, I think, and ultimately, concede while giving Crow a nod.

"I'm serious," he says while still holding my arm. "I need to hear you promise me now that I know you can talk."

"I promise," I say aloud and add a nod for comfort.

Crow holds my gaze for another moment before turning and continuing down the trail. "Your mother and father meant a lot to me," he says calmly. "When I was very young, the lawmen in Oklahoma killed my family and put me in jail for no real reason. Your father worked with the lawmen on behalf of Dutch and when he saw me in there, he bartered my release and brought me home with him. Him and your mom took good care of me. They fed me, dressed me, taught me how to read and write."

His breathing is heavy now, and I can sense the emotion in his voice. "I owe my life to your father, and we will make this right. I promise." He stops and once again turns to face me. "I promise we will make him pay for everything. We just need to be smart about it and we need Patrick to guide us."

I nod in agreement, and we continue forward. Curving and climbing as we make our way through the hills while both of us remain quiet. After another fifteen minutes, we arrive at the mouth of our cavern. I lay my load on the ground and begin removing the tree limbs we used to disguise the opening. Once finished, I climb underneath and roll the cart backward as close as I can to the entrance.

"Lay the blankets in the cart." Crow says, still holding onto Emma and waiting patiently.

I walk over and unroll the blankets from around the rifle. I place them in the bottom of the cart and put the knapsack to the front. Crow gently lays Emma in the cart and positions her body so that her head is resting on the knapsack and her legs are sticking out the back of the cart with her knees bent over the top.

I stretch my arms out to the side and arch my back inward in an attempt to loosen the cramps I am feeling in my body from carrying the load all this way. Crow is already pushing the cart down the tracks, so I grab my rifle and hustle to catch up, doing so just as he reaches the doors. I wait as Crow leans over the cart to untie the doors, readying my rifle just in case.

It is pitch black inside. Crow reaches next to him

and pulls a lantern off the wall, strikes a match, and lights it. He continues forward into the cavern and lights multiple lanterns as I stand and lazily watch him. Once he returns to the cart, he reaches in and gently scoops Emma up and carries her to the straw bed in the corner. I pick up the blankets and knapsack before eventually following him. As he lays her down, her lifeless body falls limply, with arms sprawling out to the side and legs crossed at the knees. Crow straightens her up, lifts the shirt, and unravels the bedsheet.

"Make a fire a few feet over there," he says while pointing just off to the side of the straw bed and his voice echoing off the rock of the cave.

With each load of firewood I carry, I peek around Crow and watch as he delicately cleans and dresses her wound. It is cold in here; I feel. It will be nice to have a fire if we're just going to sit here and wait. Once I feel I have enough wood, I retrieve a jug of moonshine and pour it over the wood, just as Uncle Jack showed me earlier in the day. I strike a match and toss it on top, jumping back as the burst of flames bounds outward and comes surprisingly close to Crow's head. He doesn't falter as he finishes wrapping the sheet around Emma's body and covers her with blankets. I move next to him as reaches up and wipes her auburn hair behind her ear before placing the back of his hand on her forehead.

"She's burning up." He says while standing to his feet and peering at her nervously.

I look down at her. You can see her chest slightly heaving as she breathes through a closed mouth. Her cheeks, yet milky white, have a reddish glow and I still think she is beautiful.

While I sit there staring at her, Crow had gone

down to the brook and filled a pail with water. When he returns, he kneels by her side and, while pulling down on her chin to open her mouth, pours small amounts of water from a ladle. He then takes his fingers, dips it in the water and rubs it on her lips. While leaning back on his knees, he dips the ladle again and drank from it, himself. When satisfied, he dips it again, but this time, passes it to me. I drink and realize just how thirsty I am. The water is refreshing. I dunk it again in the water and take another long drink before returning the ladle to the pail and waiting for Crow to make the next move.

Crow walks over and tosses more wood on the fire. "Make sure to add plenty of wood to the fire before you go to sleep, so it'll make it through the night," he says, while making eye contact with me. "Just not too big that you'll catch fire."

"Aren't you staying?" I ask him, clearly confused by his statement.

"Can't. I have to get rid of the horse and I want to find Sean. We will need him. This is very serious, Cieran." Crow leans his hand out and places it on my shoulder. "You'll be OK here," he continues. "No one knows this place is here, and I'll be back in a couple of hours. Try to get some rest."

I nod in agreement, even though I don't want to be alone. It would be nice to have Sean here, I agree. I always feel safe with him. Crow holds my gaze for another moment before pulling his hand away and turning back toward the door. Within an instant, he is back at the cavern and closing the door behind him.

I stand there for a minute, watching the doors and hoping Crow will come back inside. Almost immediately, a sense of loneliness washes over me. I look around the dimly lit cave and watch as the glow of the lanterns dance on the walls. I sit down next to Emma and stare at her. She looks peaceful, I think. I pick up the knapsack and start pulling the items out. There is ham wrapped in a rag, biscuits in another, and jerky in a third. I lay the jerky to the side and pick up a biscuit, crack it in half and add a piece of ham between the two pieces. The ham is cut thick and oddly shaped. I wrap the rest of the ham and biscuits and lay them on the bed next to the jerky. I take a bite of the biscuit. It tastes good and I realize I am starving. I haven't eaten since this morning, and this is truly needed.

While holding the biscuit in one hand, I pull a blanket out of the knapsack and place it over my legs. I watch the fire dance across the logs as I sit there and eat. I can hear my chewing along with the cracking and popping of the fire and feel a total sense of loneliness wash over me. Barely thinking about anything and seemingly content with the silence. Once I finish, I drink another ladle of water and move the pail off the bed, closer toward the fire.

As I lay back, I position the knapsack under my head as a pillow. It still holds another blanket, but it's really not much of a pillow, I believe. I pull the blanket up to my neck and reach over to take Emma's hand in mine. I don't look at her, instead I return my gaze to the fire and continue watching flames dance across the logs. Off in the distance, I can hear water running from the brook before focusing my attention on the sound of the fire crackling next to me. Within minutes, my eyes close and I fall fast asleep.

That night, in a lonely cave while lying next to a stranger

that will surely die, I dreamed. I dreamt of Emma and how much we are in love. We are fishing together, eating together, running through the streets, playing and always together. Constantly smiling, yet never speaking. My parents are there. Patrick, Sean, Ryan, Sara, Uncle Jack, all there. They're all speaking and laughing with one another, yet Emma and I never speak. We are content holding hands and smiling at one another. I am happy. Gone is the anger and resentment I feel for Bobby Kelly. Gone is the loneliness and the restlessness I have grown accustomed to in my daily life. I am at peace, and it feels great. I wish I could have stayed in that dream place forever. But all good things must come to an end and eventually, I open my eyes.

I lay there for a moment and close my eyes, stretching in place and doing my best to stay within the dream. It is quickly fading from memory and while I try to hold on as long as I can; the feeling disappears, and I open my eyes to face the day. It is much darker now and I wonder how long I have been asleep. Most of the lanterns are burnt out, and the fire is barely visible. Only ash and red embers remain. I stand up, realizing my shoes are still on my feet, and glance toward Emma for a moment. She has remained in the same position all night and still looks to be at peace.

I scurry off behind one of the stills to use the restroom. I know Emma is still unconscious, but it still feels like the right thing to do. After I relieve myself, I collect a large armload of wood and add it to the fire. I douse it with a large shot of moonshine and watch as it immediately bursts back into flames. I can feel the heat on my face and take a step back. Where is Crow, I wonder? Maybe I haven't been asleep as long as I think

I have.

Kneeling by Emma's side, I place the back of my hand on her forehead. Warm but not hot. I slide the blanket down and lift her shirt, exposing the sheet tied around her stomach. Carefully, I unwrap the sheet, exposing the wound. It is filled with a yellow substance but not bleeding anymore. I pick up the moonshine and dribble a little over the wound, which instantly turns the yellow paste into a white for some reason. Using a clean rag, I wipe away the substance, adding more moonshine periodically. I don't know how much to use, I just believe it can't hurt. It takes a few minutes, but I finally clear everything from the wound and can see a small incision that is pink in color. I douse my hands in moonshine and apply a layer from each container. Each cream, when combined with one other, makes a yellow paste that smells sort of sweet but also sour. I cover it with gauze and again wrap the sheet around her. I cover her with a blanket and pull the pail of water close. Just as I had seen Crow do, I pull her chin down and pour in a few drops of water. I also dip my fingers and wipe them on her lips. Her lips are soft and I can't help but notice how bright pink they are. I worry to myself that the water may taste like moonshine from washing my hands. I take a drink myself and feel the coolness of the water as it slides down my throat. It tastes great, so I take another one before finally standing to my feet.

Walking to the doors of the cave, I again wonder when Crow would return. Hopefully, Sean will be with him and we can figure this out so I can go home. I open the doors and start down the cavern a short way before noticing the light glistening off the tracks and as I step out; I realize daylight had recently come.

141

Panicking, I walk to the edge of the hill and look around for any sign of Crow. Where is he, I wonder? I stand there for a few minutes, squinting off in the distance and searching for his movement. Hesitantly, I turn and head back down the tunnel to the cave. I immediately go to work filling the lanterns with oil and adding extra wood to the fire. I retrieve the jerky, place it in my pocket, and take another drink of water. As I exit the doors, I peer back at Emma and worry about her being left alone. Shaking my head in disbelief, I close the doors and latch them, locking her inside.

I collect the tree limbs, placing them one by one over the opening until it is disguised. Taking a bite of jerky, I jog down the hill toward the trails. As I chew, I think to myself that I probably shouldn't be eating while I run and put the jerky back in my pocket. While retrieving my hand from my pocket, I realize I have forgotten my pistol and my rifle. Stopping dead in my tracks, I turn back toward the cave. I reason with myself that I don't need them since I won't be gone long and probably shouldn't risk Sean taking them from me after he finds out what I've done. I concede to myself and turn, once again jogging down the trails toward home.

As I twist my way through the trails, I think about how I will get my revenge on Bobby Kelley. Once Sean gets involved, I am likely going to have to explain to him what happened to Emma and, consequently, what I heard. While he is busy getting Emma to a doctor, I think, I can sneak back to the Kelley's house and get him. My thoughts get away from me as I consider many scenarios that all lead to the death of Bobby Kelley. I am calm and feel jubilation as I envision the image of his bloody body lying dead on the floor.

Popping out of the tree line, I veer left toward the road, deciding there is no reason for me to cross the meadowlands this time since there is no need to hide and it will only slow me down. I pick up speed while running down the road, since I'm not having to twist and turn through the trails. Within minutes, I arrive at the bottoms and feel comfort wash over me. As I turn left to go up the hill toward our house, I notice people moving around in that direction and are shouting to each other and seem to be bothered by something. None of them notice me as I peak the top of the hill and lay eyes on my house.

Off in the near distance, a dozen cars are lined from our house through Crow's front yard. My heart flutters and my stomach churns as I stop and stare in disbelief. I'm in trouble, I think and don't know what to do. I think about turning around and going back to the cave, but realize my feet have already started walking toward the house. What am I doing? They will take me to jail if I go up there. My body feels a range of emotions as I reason with myself to run. I am afraid; I am relieved; I am sad, and I continue forward. I don't want to go to jail and will miss my family; I worry. How will I ever get my revenge on Bobby Kelley if I'm in jail? My brothers, I reason. I will tell my brothers what happened, and they will kill him.

A sense of peace passes over me as I walk the short distance from the road into our yard. Not a soul is looking at me, and I notice at least a dozen men with rifles. All are yelling and pointing their rifles at Crow's house. As I round the corner, I can clearly see Crow standing on his front porch with a rifle in one hand and a large knife in the other. He is calm, yet has a stern look

143

on his face. As I edge closer, a hand reaches around my arm and pulls me into their arms.

"Come over here, lad," Uncle Jack says as he walks me behind a car and out of the open.

My gaze is fixed on Crow as he shouts loudly at the men who surround him. All at once, he jumps off of his porch and takes off, running toward the group of men yelling some sort of war cry. A hail of gunfire erupts, cutting Crow down after only a few steps. Uncle Jack fell to the ground and releases his grip on me. There are still men firing shots as I sprint across the yard and fall to my knees at Crow's side. His body is bullet ridden and his shirt is turning red. His face is somber as blood dribbles from the corner of his mouth and drips down his chin.

He recognizes me and smiles as he lifts his hand to my cheek. "I have repaid my debt to your father," he mumbles as his hand stops and slides down from my cheek, falling limp at his side.

Chapter 8

The Secret Revealed

As the men close in around us, I am jerked to my feet and being carried back toward our house.

"Come on Cieran," Sean calls out as he drags me away.

I fight only for a moment as sadness washes over me and I grow weak with despair. I walk clumsily with Sean as I peer back at Crow through the crowd that has encircled his lifeless body. Within moments, I recognize Bobby Kelley has walked up alongside the group and is shouting at them ferociously.

"Now what have you done?" he yells while flailing his arms in the air. "We will never find her."

Digging my feet in the ground, I lunge backward out of Sean's grasp. I am able to take two steps toward Bobby before I am once again lifted off my feet and securely gripped in Sean's arms. I am gritting and growling as I twist and fight to break free but trapped within a stronger man's arms.

"Stop it!" Sean yells as he grips harder, his fingers digging into my skin, and continues walking toward the house. "He's gone."

I fight back with all my might, kicking and clawing, while trying to break free from Sean's grasp, but I'm unable to as he carries me up the porch steps and into our living room. Uncle Jack follows and begins pleading with me to calm down as Sean sits me on the sofa. I stand up and Sean pushes down on my forehead, putting me back down on the sofa.

"Get ahold of him!" he yells at Uncle Jack as he sits down next to me.

Uncle Jack places his arms around me and holds me tight. "Calm down, boy," he pleads sternly while fastening his grip.

I push back, but I'm unable to wiggle free, as I have severely underestimated Uncle Jack's strength.

"I'm going to find out what's going on," Sean says as he disappears out the door.

Sara joins us on the couch, sitting next to me, and I am sandwiched between the two of them. I can feel tears spilling down my cheeks as I twist and jerk with all my strength. One of my hands comes free and connects with the side of Sara's face. I hear her wince as she lifts her hands to cover up and protect herself. As I stare into her eyes, I see that I have hurt her and feel all emotion leave my body. I immediately stop fighting and lean back, wrapping my arms around her, and burst into tears. She forgives me quickly and places her arms around me. We sit there together for a minute, holding each other with both of us weeping. Crow is like family to all of us and it hurts to see him gunned down in front of our eyes. Uncle Jack sits here next to us and rubs my back as I finally relent, accepting the situation and finding solace in the arms of my loved ones.

After a few minutes, I calmly stand and walk to the screen door before finally stepping out onto the porch. Uncle Jack follows and Sara stands at the door as we sadly watch the people move about in Crow's yard. Twenty yards off the corner of the porch and behind our truck stands Sean, Dutch Kelley, and Captain Lewis. Sean is leaning on the bed of the truck with Dutch at his side and Captain Lewis standing directly in front of him, waving his hands around as he speaks.

"You have to know something!" Captain Lewis yells out aggressively.

Sean is calm and has his arms crossed in front of him despite how he must feel. "I got home just a little while ago," Sean replies sternly. "I've been down at the roadhouse all night. I don't know what's going on. I was asleep when all this happened."

"You O'Connors'!" Captain Lewis yells again, this time pointing his finger in Sean's face. "You have to know something."

Sean steps forward toward Captain Lewis and his eyes go dark. "I know your men just killed my best friend." He states matter-of-factly.

Captain Lewis doesn't back down and presses his body against Sean's. It is a weak effort as he is much shorter and smaller than Sean. Even Captain Lewis knows not to mess with him. Sean is tough and everyone knows there is a darkness inside him that is not to be underestimated. His fist grips tightly as he drops his arms to his side. "Crow would've never done what you said!" he yells at the top of his lungs.

Captain Lewis, while still scowling, steps back to give Sean some room. "When was the last time you saw Crow?" he asks, seeming to calm a bit but still not backing down.

"I already told you," Sean says loudly. "Yesterday evening before I left to make deliveries and then I went to the roadhouse. I was with Betsy Miller all night. You can ask her yourself."

Dutch Kelley lifts his arm and places it on Sean's shoulder. "I want my granddaughter back," he mutters softly but still speaks sternly. "Where is Patrick?"

Sean relaxes a little and leans back again to rest on the bed of the truck. "Went to Kansas City on business yesterday." He says, while turning his attention to Dutch.

Dutch clenches his jaw before continuing. "When's he coming home?"

"Tomorrow," Sean replies quickly.

Dutch doesn't seem to care about the answer as he continues staring at Sean. "Why would this man kidnap my daughter?" He asks, as if Sean had the answer.

"I don't think he would," Sean replies as he softens his tone. "I've known that man almost my whole life and he would never do anything like that."

"A shirtless man fitting his description was spotted with a body draped over my stolen horse in the park last night." Dutch yells back wildly. "They followed their tracks here and the O'Briens' said they saw him riding through their yard." He stops for a moment and takes a breath before continuing, "He wouldn't let us anywhere near the house and charged at us like a wild man. Once Captain Lewis got into the house after he was shot, there are blood droplets in the living room." Dutch grabs Sean by the arm and attempts to pull him close. "Now I want to know what is going on."

Sean pulls away from him and steps sideways, preparing himself for battle. "I already said that I don't know."

Dutch clenches his jaw again and peers back over toward Crow's house. He holds his gaze on the men moving around in the yard for a moment before scanning back toward our house and stops once he sees us standing on the porch. "What about them?" he asks, nodding in our direction. "Did you folks see anything last night?" He shouts loud enough for us to hear.

Uncle Jack clears his throat. Stuttering slightly, he replies, "Uh, I was piss drunk last night and slept like a rock. I didn't see anything until you folks showed up this morning."

Dutch is unamused with Uncle Jack's statement and moves his gaze toward the door, consequently awaiting Sara's response and staring directly into her eyes.

"Nah, no, nothing," she responds softly, and I know that she's still crying and having a tough time responding.

Dutch stands there for a moment, staring back and forth between Sara and Uncle Jack, yet never even looks at me.

"I'll go question them," Captain Lewis says while stepping toward the house.

Sean moves over in front to cut him off. "You heard 'em say they didn't see anything. No need to bother them any further."

Once again, Captain Lewis pushes forward into Sean. "I'll do anything I damn well please," he responds while glaring at Sean and doing his best to assert dominance.

In the blink of an eye, Sean grabs Captain Lewis under the armpits, lifting him almost completely off his feet to where only the tips of his toes are scraping the ground. "I don't think you will," he says sternly and is ready to fight.

Evan Blake walks up and pulls a pistol from under his jacket, points it directly at Sean's face. Sean let go of Captain Lewis, dropping him back to the ground and almost causing him to fall while turning his attention to Evan.

"What do you wanna do?" Sean asks as more of a statement than a question while stepping directly in front of Evan.

"Put that away," Dutch says as he waves his hand at Evan. "Where is Bobby?" he asks blindly.

Captain Lewis steps backward and straightens his jacket as Evan continues to stare at Sean. "He's in the house," Evan answers while slowly putting his gun back in the holster and without breaking eye contact with Sean.

I have grown uneasy as their conversation has gotten more tense, and I now realize I have moved off the porch a few feet in their direction. As I hear that Bobby Kelley is close, I ignore them and look toward Crow's house, searching for him. I can feel the blood pulsing through my veins and my body grows anxious as I hope I can exact my revenge. I turn and start walking in his direction when, all of a sudden, a car skids to a stop and a man jumps out.

"We found the horse tied up down the road a couple miles," he yells out, drawing everyone's attention. "It's right in front of an old shack. Got a man keeping watch till we get back."

"Let's go!" Dutch shouts without a moment of hesitation as he turns away from Sean and walks toward one of the cars.

Without any further direction, all the men scamper about and pile into cars as Evan Blake runs past me into Crow's house. Within moments, Bobby Kelley steps out of the house and is walking quickly toward one of the cars. I change direction and start walking toward him, not knowing what I will do and feeling as if I'm not in control of my body. I am moving quickly, but not fast enough as he jumps in a car and speeds off down the road and out of sight.

I am still staring off down the road when I realize Sean is standing next to me. I look over at him as he stares at the ground and sorrow covers his face. I follow his gaze and find that we are standing next to Crow, as he has not yet been moved. Looking at his perished and blood-soaked body brings sadness over me once again. This is my fault, I think to myself. He died because of me. He could have told them what I did and saved himself, but he didn't. He protected me. I begin to cry again as I think about what he'd done. Sean doesn't hug me, nor does he cry. He just stands there staring at Crow, lying lifeless on the ground.

"I'll call the undertaker," Uncle Jack says as he walks up beside us. He is carrying a blanket and passes one side to Sean. "Here, help me cover the man up."

As the two of them cover Crow, I turn and walk back toward the house. Sara swings the screen door open and steps out.

"I need you to tell me about last night." She says as I continue walking past the front porch.

I don't stop and take off in a jog, headed toward the road.

"Cieran!" She yells from behind me. "Cieran,

151

come back!"

Weaving my way through the trails, I feel the burning in my legs as I steadily climb the hills back toward the cave. Every muscle in my body tensed with each twist and turn in the road. Sweat seeps through my clothing and my breath is hot and dries my lips. Gone are my tears. I am driven once again by rage, desiring the opportunity to extinguish Bobby Kelley's life. I have no fear of anything as I visualize the images of him killing my parents. I just watched as Crow was gunned down in the yard and imagine Bobby as the only one pulling the trigger. I have to get him. Filling the overwhelming urge to confront him is creating tremendous anxiety and I feel as if I will explode. My heart is racing as I top the hill and face the entrance to the cave. Without hesitation, I sling the tree limbs to the side and dart down the tunnel, slowing only for a moment as I fiddle with the latch before finally bursting inside. Instantly, I see the face of Emma as she has moved from the straw bed and is crawling toward the door.

"Help," she begs softly while reaching her hand out.

I stop dead in my tracks as I gaze surprisingly down upon her. She has scooted ten yards from the bed and is half lying on her stomach and half on her side with her hand extended out towards me. Her hair is stringy and offers barely a glimpse of her fear-filled eyes. I walk toward her and, while taking her hand, kneel down, offering support as she slides her body around, trying to sit up. She is weak and unable to complete the maneuver, so I roll her over and reach one arm under her legs and the other around her back. She concedes and wraps her arms around my shoulders. As I lift, my body contorts forward and my legs wobble under her dead weight. I grunt as I thrust with all my strength, standing directly upright.

"No," she yells, horrified. "It's you!"

Glancing down at her face, I recognize the sheer terror in her eyes as she wiggles. I take a labored step toward the bed as she musters all her energy and begins silently screaming while also pounding at my body with her left arm. As I take a second step, she lifts her arm that was clutching to my shoulder and claws at my right eye. With her fingernails digging into the corner, I wince from the extreme pain and allow my left arm to slip from around her back. I dramatically try to grab onto her as she tumbles to the floor, landing firmly on the back of her head, and sounds as if a small caliber pistol was fired. I kneel down, bringing her legs to rest on the floor as she moans softly and rolls her head back and forth. Her eyes blink slowly, and she seems to mumble something. I take her hand in mine as she lets out a deep breath and mutters softly, "Don't kill me."

Her eyelids flutter a few more times before completely closing. I rub my hand across her forehead and move her hair to the side as I lean close to her ear and whisper softly, "I won't hurt you ever again."

I sit there for a moment, staring at her unconscious body, not able to understand how, once again, I have hurt her. I can't believe it. My face is burning hot, and I feel stinging from the corner of my eye. I close it tightly and detect a droplet of blood as it rolls down my cheek. Lifting my hand, I wipe the blood away and caress around my eye to assess the damage. The pain is piercing as my finger brushes across loose tissue. My eye is watering profusely, but it's nothing major, only a slight cut as she had dug away the skin. I wipe away the blood again and clean my fingers by wiping them across my trousers before lifting Emma's head by placing my hand on the back of her neck and gently lifting. I run my fingers down the back of her head, stopping once I reach the knot and recognize the dampness, assuming that it must be blood.

While rolling her body to the side, I run my finger through her hair to inspect the damage. Just a slight cut and a tiny amount of blood. I immediately roll her onto her back and position myself to pick her up again. This time, I do not have the support of her arm around my shoulders and labor as I struggle to stand to my feet. As I lift, I clench her tightly, not wanting to drop her again. Once to my feet, I shuffle cautiously toward the bed. Still feeling the sting, I close my eye and feel another droplet of blood squeeze out and roll down my cheek.

Arriving at the straw bed, I kneel but feel my body give out. I quickly roll to the side, allowing Emma's body to brace securely against mine. Air shoots from my mouth as I exhale deeply when our bodies hit the bed and Emma falls directly on top of me. My arms still wrap around her back and legs, cradling her as if she were a baby while I lay there for a moment. I hold her loosely while trying to catch my breath. Eventually, her body slides off mine and her head comes to a rest on my shoulder. Her legs are crossed over mine and I continue lying there, breathing heavily and content to be still. As I calm myself, I can hear her breathing softly and, for a moment, I am at peace.

Although I feel comfortable resting next to her with our limbs touching, I also have a guilty feeling that

I cannot shake. I have done this to her. My actions cause her suffering, and I am at fault for Crow's death. If only I hadn't gone to the Kelleys' last night, I think. She would still be cozy in her home and Crow would be alive. We would probably be here right now, only we would be making moonshine instead of hiding a young girl. I lay there for a moment, imagining Uncle Jack and me moving about, making his special elixir.

"No." I say aloud. If that is the case, then I would never have known the truth about my parents and I wouldn't have known that Bobby Kelley murdered them. And just like that, I dismiss the sensitive feeling and slide out from under her. While I position her body up on a pillow and straighten her out, I once again feel the back of her head. The knot has increased in size a little, but the blood ceases to flow. Instead, it is replaced with a partial scab that I carefully touch, but make sure not to break loose. I can still feel the soreness around my eye and caress it with the tip of my finger. It also has scabbed over, but my eye continues to water.

Once again, I load wood on the fire and fill the lanterns. They don't need as much fuel as before since I haven't been gone very long. I refill the water bowl, taking a long drink for myself before collecting the knapsack. I put the biscuits and ham by the water bowl and pull the jerky from my pocket. Wiping away the lint, I place it on top of the other wrapped food for Emma. While covering her with the blanket, I take a moment to gaze at her face. I will miss you, I think to myself. I am sorry.

Dismissing my concern, I quickly stand and retrieve my satchel. I pull the pistol from inside, stick it in my pocket where the jerky had been moments earlier, and pull out the picture of Emma. I unfold it and stare at her image for a moment before placing it in my left pocket. I sling the satchel over my head to my shoulder and pick up my rifle. Taking a deep breath, I turn toward the door, ready to face my task and excited to do so. Before I can even take my first step, the door opens, and Sean pokes his head inside.

Every muscle in my body freezes, and I stand as still as a statue while he enters the cave.

"Cieran, what's going on?" he asks while walking cautiously toward me.

Concern covers his face and as he slowly makes his way toward me, he continually scans the room as if he is looking for something. Sean steps directly in front of me and peers deeply into my eyes. Placing a hand on each of my shoulders, he gently moves me to the side while slowly turning his attention to Emma lying nestled on the bed.

His hands fall from my shoulders and hang limp at his side. "Oh, my God!" He exclaims.

Still staring at Emma, he asks, "What is this? Is this why Sara said you didn't come home last night?"

I stand there watching Sean stare down at her. His mouth has fallen open, and his forehead is drawn as if he is pondering a complex question. He kneels beside her and hesitantly brushes the back of his hand across her forehead. He glances momentarily back up at me, then returns his gaze to Emma as he lowers the blanket. The shirt she is wearing has lifted a little and exposes the underside of Crow's makeshift bandage. Without hesitation, he lifts the shirt and unties the bandage. Using no care or caution, Sean unwraps the bed sheet and removes the gauze. He sits there for a moment as if frozen in time, staring at the wound that is covered in yellow paste before finally replacing the gauze and wrapping the bed sheet back around her.

Once finished, he slides the blanket to her neck and pivots off his knees before coming to rest on his bottom next to Emma. He has not looked in my direction and still stares at her while asking, "What the hell is goin' on?"

While I watch as Sean searches for an answer in his mind, I feel tears well up in my eyes once again. "It was an accident," I mumble aloud.

I am shocked to hear the words come out of my mouth, but not nearly as much as Sean. He whips his head around and stares directly into my eyes while shifting his body back to his knees. Reaching up for me, he replies softly, "Cieran. You talked."

All at once, I drop my rifle and fall to my knees in front of him. I bury my head in his arms and start to cry.

Sean wraps his arms around me and hugs tightly. He caresses the back of my head, slowly running his fingers through my hair. The salt from my tears burn as they run across the scratch given to me by Emma. We sit there for a long moment, holding each other as I let out all the emotion that is burning inside me. I haven't cried for a long time, but over the last twenty-four hours; I feel as if I have made up for lost time.

As my sobbing trails off, Sean pushes himself backward and peers down at my face. "Tell me what happened," he says calmly.

Leaning back, I wipe the tears from my face, wincing slightly as my hand brushes across the scrape on my eye. I stare directly into his eyes and observe nothing but love coming back to me. Taking a deep breath, I begin, "I saw her at the meeting with Dutch."

Sean watches me intently and hangs on my every word as I tell him how I snuck off to Dutch's house, hoping to see her. His face grows tight lipped, and a scowl crosses his face as I described laying in the bushes and overhearing Bobby Kelley relive the murder of our parents. He stays silent as the words pour out of me. His breathing is heavy, and I know he is listening to what I say.

"She popped up behind me and startled me. I stabbed her before I knew what I was doing," I continue. "It was an accident."

Before I can say another word, Sean stands to his feet and pulls me up with him. "Get your gun," he says firmly. "We're gettin' out of here and going home before they come back."

While I pick up my rifle, Sean scoops Emma in his arms and heads for the door. He doesn't stop to load her into the cart. He keeps on moving down the tunnel, with me following closely. Once outside, we don't stop to cover the opening as we usually do. He is taking long strides down the hill, sloshing Emma's body back and forth as he moves, and I struggle to keep up. Once at the car, he slides her into the back seat and closes the door.

"Let's go," he shouts while motioning for me to hurry as he jumps in behind the steering wheel.

Without delay, he starts the car and pulls off while I'm still closing the door. Sean shifts gears and drives fast down the road, sliding the car around turns while barely even slowing down. He bumbles in his pocket and pulls out a pack of cigarettes, sticks one between his lips, and strikes a match. Inhaling deeply, he pulls the cigarette out of his mouth and exhales before asking, "How did Crow get involved?"

I pick up his cigarette pack and light one for myself. He glances back and forth between me and the road, watching while I work to light the cigarette. I take a drag and look at him. "That's where I went," I reply solemnly. "I stole their horse and went to Crow's. Didn't know what else to do."

Sean seems to smirk, and I don't understand why. "Did he hide you in the cave?" He asks.

I continue the story and leave no detail out as I explain to him the events leading up to this moment. "He was supposed to get you and bring you to the cave," I say in finishing the story.

Sean takes the last drag off his cigarette and flicks it out the window. "I was going to kill Bobby Kelley when you showed up," I confess.

Sean snaps his head toward me and reaches his hand out to pat my arm. "Don't you worry," he says. "We'll get that son of a bitch!"

As he slides the car into our driveway and skids to a halt, he cuts off the engine and looks all around while still sitting inside. At first, Sara steps through the screen door onto the porch with Uncle Jack following closely behind. Sean opens the car door and pops out. He walks past them and disappears into the house. Both Uncle Jack and Sara stand there on the porch, looking at the car and seeming to stare at me as I stay seated. Within moments, Sean returns carrying a blanket. He quickly surveys the surroundings before opening the door and covering Emma with the blanket. I open the car door and step out into the sunlight. While looking around, I see a couple of guys loading Crow's body into the back of a truck.

Uncle Jack climbs down off the porch and walks toward the guys. Sean closes the door to the car and watches while Uncle Jack walks up to the men and pats them on the shoulders before handing them something out of his pocket. Probably money, I think, and within a few minutes, the truck starts and pulls away before Uncle Jack walks back toward the house. With no one else around, Sean opens the door and quickly slides Emma into his arms and sprints toward the house. Sara covers her mouth with one hand while opening the screen door with the other to allow him unobstructed access to go inside.

Sara is still holding the door open as I climb the stairs and walk past her. My head is down, and I cannot look her in the eye before I follow Sean into the kitchen. He stops and allows me to catch up as he reaches the door leading to the cellar. I quickly open it and Sean sprints past me, descends the stairs, and carries Emma to a bed back in the corner.

"Pull those blankets and sheets off," he says while standing in front of the bed and still holding Emma in his arms.

I remove everything off the bed, jostling the pillow slightly as I pull the bed clothes free. Sean lays Emma on the bed, lifts her shirt, and immediately begins peeling the sheet wrapped around her stomach. As he throws the sheet on the floor, he calls out, "Sara, heat me some water, please."

I hadn't noticed, but Sara followed us to the cellar and is standing directly next to me. Upon hearing the request from Sean, she turns and climbs the stairs before disappearing into the kitchen. Sean peels off the gauze that covers her wound and reaches out to hand it to me.

Without looking up, he says to me, "go get me a jug of moonshine and fresh rags."

I hesitate for a moment, still holding the bedclothes. Sean looks over at me and shakes his hand, holding the gauze, prompting me to take it from him before repeating, "go get me a jug of moonshine and fresh rags."

I drop the bedclothes but forget to take the gauze as I turn and walk to the far wall, retrieving a jar of moonshine out of the stash we have piled in the corner. With one hand, I take the gauze from him and replace it with the jar. I climb the stairs and see Sara standing next to the stove with her hands on her hips. She looks back at me over her shoulder as I exit the room and walk into the living room. Uncle Jack is stationed by the front door, peering out the screen toward the road in front of the house. He says nothing, nor does he turn his head to acknowledge me as I speed past him into the washroom. I rush to the cabinet and retrieve a pile of wash cloths before sprinting back toward the kitchen.

Sara is still standing in front of the stove and follows me with her eyes as I quickly cross the floor before going down the stairs to the cellar. As I arrive back at Sean's side, he is kneeling at the bedside and examining Emma's wound. He reaches his hand out and takes a single washcloth from the top of the pile. Pouring a healthy dose of moonshine on the wound, he gingerly cleans away the old paste. Once clear, he adds another shot directly to the slit in Emma's stomach and pulls away as her body twists away from him. Slowly, she writhes back and forth before eventually opening her eyes.

Emma blinks repeatedly and pulls her hands

down to cover the wound. She looks at Sean wide eyed before glancing toward me. She moans and works hard to pull away, but Sean places his hand on hers and speaks softly. "It's OK, my girl." He says, "I'm trying to help."

She continues to writhe in pain but concedes as Sean moves her hands away from her stomach while proceeding to wipe at the wound. Once he is satisfied with his work, he pats her hands before standing up, trying to comfort her.

"Where am I?" She asks.

"You're safe," he replies. "No one will hurt you here."

Emma stares at him for a moment before once again turning her gaze to me. "He did this to me," she says while nodding in my direction.

I feel my face go warm as Sean speaks up. "He didn't mean to. We will tell you what happened. We just need to get you cleaned up first. I promise no one will hurt you again."

She moves her eyes to watch as Sara descends the stairs and walks toward the bed while holding a bowl of water. She sits the water bowl on the floor, passes a bar of soap to Sean, and kneels next to Emma before taking her hand in her own. "Be still, child. We'll help you," she says while whispering.

Emma grips Sara's hand, seeming to find peace with her presence as Sean dips a clean rag in the water and rubs soap on it. Sara strokes Emma's hair while humming a gospel tune as Sean cleans the wound. Although she is surrounded by strangers and even me, that hurt her. Emma lays still while Sean finishes up.

As he picks up the jar of moonshine, Sean stares

into Emma's eyes. "This will sting," he says in an understanding tone. "But it's needed."

He doesn't wait for a response and pours a shot over the freshly cleaned wound. Emma wiggles, closes her eyes, and inhales deeply as she sucks at air through her teeth until the burning finally relinquishes.

Once satisfied, Sean stands to his feet and walks toward the stairs. "Might give her a bath and some clean clothes," he says to Sara as he climbs the stairs to the top.

Sara glances over at me and nods, indicating it is time for me to leave as well. I hesitate briefly, looking at Emma's face and wanting to help somehow. She sees me looking at her and appears to shutter a bit. I recognize the fear in her eyes, so I immediately turn and walk upstairs, closing the cellar door behind me.

As I walk into the living room, I see Uncle Jack is still standing by the door, peering outside. He turns his head and gives me a fake smile but does not speak. Sean is pacing back and forth across the living room floor and upon seeing me, he stops and turns back toward the kitchen.

"Come with me," he orders.

I follow him through the kitchen and out the back door toward the shed. I watch as he lifts a few boards in the floor before pulling three boxes and places them next to my feet. Kneeling next to one box, he lifts the lid and exposes a multitude of guns and ammunition. I am taken aback at the sight, since I didn't even know they were there. He moves on to a second box, opens it up and for the first time in my life, I see two tommy guns with rolls of ammunition. I have seen them in the picture shows and know what they are. They can fire a lot of bullets quickly and I have always wanted to shoot one.

While opening the third box, my mind is pulled back from visualizing shooting the tommy gun as I see this box is mostly filled with cash. More money than I've ever seen in my short life. How did I not know they were here? I wonder?

"Help me take them inside," he says after closing the lid.

I don't move. I swallow the lump in my throat before asking sheepishly, "Is she going to be OK?"

Sean glances up at me and relaxes a bit. While nodding his head, he replies, "She'll be OK. As long as we keep it from getting infected."

"What are we going to do?" I ask, ashamed of the position I've put us in.

Standing to his feet, he replies. "I don't know yet. They're for sure coming back and we need Patrick home. If they find her in the cellar, they'll kill all of us. Hell, they may do it anyway if they don't get some answers about Crow."

Sadness returns over me as I remember his bullet filled body lying lifeless on the ground. "It's my fault," I mutter despairingly.

Sean steps directly in front of me and places his hand on my shoulder, cupping the back of my head. "Yes, it is," he says softly. "We all have consequences for our actions and this one is yours."

I drop my eyes to the floor and feel ashamed to look at him.

"But" he continues. "We're O'Connors' and we stick together. We'll figure this out as a family."

He drops his hand away from me and grabs the smaller box, sitting it on top of one of the larger ones. "Come on now, grab an end. We don't have all day."

We don't speak anymore as we make two trips to carry the boxes inside, placing them in the living room. Sean immediately opens the boxes and starts placing guns around the house, even passing a shotgun to Uncle Jack as he stands watch by the door. Uncle Jack asks no questions and seems to understand the situation as he places it on the floor next to him. He is uncharacteristically stone faced and simply turns back toward the door, peering out toward the road.

While Sean works, I simply stand in the middle of the living room, unable to move. He hasn't asked for my help, and I haven't volunteered. After a few minutes, the sound of a door closing from the kitchen attracts all three of our attention and we watch as Sara enters the room and takes a seat on the sofa, positioning her hands in front of her coming to rest on her lap.

"I got her washed up and in one of my nightgowns." She says, breaking the silence. "I put what medicine I had on her wound and gave her something to help her sleep."

"Good," Sean replies as he walks next to Sara and peers down at her.

"Her head is banged up in a couple of spots," she continues. "But I think she'll be alright. She's confused and scared."

I am watching Sara while she speaks, recognizing the sympathy she feels for Emma. I also notice that she hasn't taken her eyes off me since walking into the room and I can feel the flushness rise on my face and my palms sweat.

"Now, does someone want to tell me what is going on?" she asks with a worried expression crossing her face.

Sean starts to answer, "Cieran went to...."

"I did it!" I blurt out.

Chapter 9

The Searching

The words shoot from my mouth as if they are bullets. Uncle Jack turns and stares at me with his mouth gaped open while Sara leaps to her feet and walks up to me. Bewildered, she wraps her arms around me and hugs tightly. I don't hug her back and she quickly lets go while also stepping away.

"I wanted to see her and went to the Kelley's house," I continue without pause. "While I was there, I overheard Bobby Kelley talk about killing mom and dad."

Sara's hands fly upward to cover her mouth and Uncle Jack takes a seat on the sofa, appearing lifeless. For the third time, the three of them sit there and listen as I tell what happened. I spare no detail and feel as if my soul has left my body while reciting my account of that evening and the moments leading up to now. All emotion is gone as I stand there listening to myself speak. My body language is frail, and I can feel my feet tingle. As I speak, all three are intrenched in the story. Even Sean appears as if he has never heard it before while hanging on to every word.

When I finish, the entire room remains quiet for a

few minutes before Uncle Jack finally clears his throat to speak. "You know, it now appears to me I might have heard a car pull up that night." He swallows a lump in his throat as tears well in his eyes. "I thought it was your father," he says softly. "I thought it was odd when the second car pulled up a bit later but was too drunk to get up and look."

Uncle Jack wipes his eyes and plucks a jug of moonshine off the floor. After taking a drink, he continues. "If I hadn't been drunk, maybe I could've saved 'em."

A teardrop falls from his eye and Sara walks over, sits next to him on the sofa, and puts her arm around his shoulder.

"It's not your fault, Uncle Jack." Sean says in support. "Never could've seen that coming."

Uncle Jack takes another swig off the jar and leans back, trying to regain his composure. "What do we do now?" He asks.

Sean walks around and stares out the screen door. "I don't know," he replies. "If they find her here, they'll kill us all. There's no way to get her back to them without them finding out that Cieran took her. They're gonna be all over this area lookin' for her when they find out she's not at that shack that Crow left the horse in front of."

"Bless his heart," Uncle Jack mutters. "He must've known they'd be all over his place."

We all sit there for a moment, most likely all thinking of Crow and his ultimate sacrifice. They're probably all mad at me, I think to myself. "I didn't mean to get him involved," I say aloud, not knowing what else to say.

They all look at me before Sara once again rises

and walks over to me. While wrapping her arms around me, she whispers in my ear. "It's not your fault."

Of course, I know she is lying. We all know it is my fault.

"If he hadn't done that, I would've never gotten Cieran home safely," Sean states. "They would all still be here and combing the bottoms if he hadn't got them to go on a wild goose chase." He pauses for a moment, as if in thought. "It's important we're all together until Patrick gets home." Turning around to face us, he continues, "If we can get past the next couple of days, then this thing gets easier."

I shrug away from Sara and step toward him. "I'll take her back," I say. "I'll tell them it was me."

"They'll kill you," he replies. "There's no way out of this right now. We just need to wait."

"But..." I interject.

"No," Sean says while cutting me off. "We must keep them out of here and away from the cellar. That's the plan for now."

Sara walks to the sofa and sits down, places her hands over her face, and begins to cry.

"It'll be OK, Sara," Sean says while trying to comfort her.

None of us find peace in his statement and it shows on our faces. Even Sean doesn't believe it will be OK, I feel. This is bad. I think for a minute about what my brothers would do if they ever found out I was missing. They'd be everywhere and wouldn't stop until they found me. I'm sure the Kelley's feel the same way when it comes to Emma.

At first, one car pulls up out front, then I can hear car after car. Each one stopping, cutting the engine, and

I hear their doors closing. The light murmur of men talking sounds off in the distance, and I imagine them walking around while searching for clues. Eventually, I hear a car pull up in our driveway, very close to the house.

"Here we go," Sean says while adjusting his pistol in the back of his trousers before stepping through the screen door and out onto the porch.

Uncle Jack stands to his feet and picks up the shotgun while motioning for me to do the same. He then steps back out of view of the screen door. I adjust the pistol in my pocket so that the handle sticks out the side before finally picking up my rifle. Sara stands up and walks toward the kitchen, slinking behind the doorway while also peering out around the corner. I catch a slight glimmer of metal as she positions herself behind the wall and think to myself that even she has a weapon, now we are all ready.

"Dutch, you find her?" Sean asks, already knowing the answer.

"Nah, my boy," I hear in response. The voice is seeded in a deep Irish accent I know is definitely Dutch's. "Bloody rags all over the place, so it doesn't look good."

"I'm sure she's OK," Sean responds.

"Ah, and what makes you so sure?" Dutch asks angrily.

I cannot see his face, but I can imagine the gritting teeth and Dutch's evil eyes staring at Sean.

"I'm not," Sean says. "Just trying to stay positive."

I hear more footsteps walk up to join them.

"I want to know what's going on and I want to

know now!"

The voice that calls out is forever burned in my memory, and I know it is Bobby Kelley. I grip the rifle at both ends and raise it toward the door with my finger on the trigger. I can burst through the door and kill him right now, I think. He'll never see it coming. I quickly dismiss the idea, as I know they will kill my family. I already have a loved one's blood on my hands, and I want no more.

"I want to know why your Indian took my daughter," Bobby asks assertively.

"I don't know Bobby," Sean replies in defense. "We're not even sure he did anything. Crow's never done anything even close to this. He protects children."

I catch a glimpse of Bobby's head as he climbs up on the porch in front of Sean. While pointing a finger in his face, Bobby yells, "I want my daughter back!"

Sean steps back two steps while replying, "I understand, but we don't know where she is."

Another man steps onto the porch, and I recognize him as Evan Blake. "Come on Bobby, relax." Evan grabs Bobby by the arm but is not looking at him. He is looking straight through the screen door at me with my rifle aiming directly at them.

"Get off me!" Bobby yells while pulling his arm from Evan's grasp. "I want answers!"

Evan grabs Bobby by the arm again and seems to flash me a smile through the door before turning his head toward Bobby. "Let's go back down here and calm down a bit, huh?"

This time, I watch as Bobby tries to pull out of Evan's grasp again, but this time, he is pulled off the porch, disappearing from my sight.

"I want to look around their house!" Bobby yells out.

"What for?" Sean asks.

"I want to see if she's in there!"

Sean shifts his weight to the side, and I can see him put his right finger in his pocket, bringing his hand closer to the gun tucked into his waistband. Seeing this causes me to grip my rifle tighter. I am already breathing heavily as I work to keep myself from shooting Bobby. I guarantee you one thing; I think. I will kill Bobby Kelley if they step through that door. Doesn't matter if they kill me too, but I am going to get him.

"You're not going in my home," Sean replies with full confidence. "There's no reason for you to. We already told you we didn't see anything."

Bobby starts to yell something else, but Dutch cuts him off.

"He's right, Bobby." Says Dutch. "We don't know anything for sure."

I hear the steps to the porch begin to creak and watch as Dutch slowly walks up to Sean and pats him on the shoulder. I move a few steps to my left so he cannot see me.

"We're gonna look around, Sean." Dutch says matter-of-factly. "I have forty men that are gonna scour this countryside looking for my granddaughter. If they find anything curious, I'm comin' in that house whether you like it or not."

With an uneasy voice, Sean responds immediately. "Go ahead Dutch. We don't have any problem with that. We hope you find her."

"Oh lad," he replies while again patting Sean's arm. "I'm not askin' for permission." He turns to walk back down the stairs but hesitates a moment before turning to face Sean once again. "Where's the Indian's body?" he asks.

"Already picked up by the undertaker," Sean replies quickly.

Dutch continues down the stairs before calling out. "Captain, send your men to examine the body."

After a moment, I hear footsteps scurry away and imagine Captain Lewis nodding his head at Dutch before following orders.

"Evan, get the men to scour every inch of this shithole neighborhood and you and Captain Lewis look through the Indian's house for clues. I want my granddaughter found tonight!"

"Yes sir," Evan responds before I hear his footsteps lead away as well.

"Come on Bobby," Dutch says. "We're goin' home. Need to let these men work."

"But Dad," Bobby interjects while sounding whiney. "I want to find Emma."

"Me too, son," he replies. "But our emotion is not gonna help 'em right now and we need to be by the phone in case they find her."

I move back close to the door, and I can see Dutch has Bobby by the arm and is leading him off toward the car parked directly in our driveway. Bobby has his head lowered and seems to carry his body like a whipped fighter as they walk.

After a few feet, Dutch turns back toward Sean. "If you hear anything, you'll be sure to give us a ring, won't ya?" He asks but before Sean had a chance to respond, he continues. "I'll be back tomorrow to visit with Patrick. Make sure he knows I'm comin'."

Without another word, the two of them walk back to their car, where Evan Blake and several other men are standing. A couple are wearing police uniforms, and the others are well dressed, but I don't recognize any of them. Bobby immediately gets in the back while Dutch speaks closely with Evan, not allowing anyone to overhear. Every so often, he looks back toward the porch where Sean is still standing and watching them. After a few minutes, he climbs in the back next to Bobby and the car backs out of the driveway before disappearing down the road.

Sean stands there on the porch for a few minutes looking around and watching the men move about before eventually coming together in Crow's yard. I can hear Evan Blake talking but can't quite make out what he is saying. He's probably giving them instructions on where to go, I think. I watched as Sean stood his ground on the porch and feel proud of him. Not once did his hand tremble, and he never faltered. I'm sure he wants to kill Bobby as much as I do, and it has to be tough for him to restrain himself with Bobby standing right next to him. As I envision the sight of Sean's hand resting on his pocket and not shaking. I realize that I also had not shaken. I feel as if I am steady handed myself and ready for a fight if they want. Feeling this also makes me proud and I kind of smile to myself.

The screen door creaks open and Sean steps through, stopping just inside the door. Sara steps into the living room from the kitchen while Uncle Jack plops down on the sofa. He lays the shotgun he is holding over his knees before taking a swig from the jug of moonshine that sits at his feet.

"Careful, Uncle Jack," Sean says as he moves over

next to me. "We need our wits about us tonight." Looking at me, he continues. "Tell me what happened after you guys' left Crow's house."

I lean my rifle against the wall and rub my sweaty palms on my trousers. "We walked to the cave," I respond. "He carried her, and I followed."

"Where at?" he asks quietly. "What direction did you go?"

I realize all the windows in the house are open and lower my voice. "Back of the property, through the tree line and across the meadowlands."

Sean nods his head. "Smart," he says confidently. "I'm sure Crow would've covered his tracks. They'll never know which way he went."

Immediately, it dawns on me. "What about mine?" I ask.

Sean looks at me quizzically as his eyebrows narrow. "What do you mean?"

"I went through the trails twice this morning," I respond. "I didn't even think about it."

I must look distraught because Sean rests his hand on my shoulder. "That's OK," he says. "They won't connect you to Crow's house or even show you were here at all. You took the road, didn't you?"

I feel a slight sense of ease and nod my head at him. Sean turns and walks next to Uncle Jack, peering once again out the screen door before collecting the jug of moonshine and having a drink himself.

"Well," says Uncle Jack, trying to break the tension. "Thought we were going to keep our wits about us?"

Sean smiles and so does Uncle Jack. Sean passes him the jug and Uncle Jack takes a swig. After wiping his face, he looks over at me before asking, "Anyone else find it peculiar this young man is talking?"

"I do," says Sara while raising her hand.

"I do too," agrees Sean.

"I mean, I'm happy about it," Sara adds.

Glancing at her, I see her smiling. Not her usual smile, but a forced smile where she probably still wants to cry, I believe.

"Anyone hungry?" she asks.

"I could eat," Uncle Jack replies.

"Might as well," says Sean.

I nod my head in agreement as Sara turns and walks into the kitchen. Without hesitation, Uncle Jack groans as he lifts himself off the sofa and we all three follow her into the kitchen, taking a seat at the table while she walks to the icebox.

"Got some ham," she says while walking back toward us carrying a plate heaping with sliced ham.

She places it on the table, retrieves a loaf of bread, and starts cutting slices. She passes me two slices and one is the heel. I hate the heel. Hell with it, I think. I'm starving and I sure don't want to put her out after all I've caused today. I take it from her and place a large piece of ham on one slice, hesitate for a moment before grabbing a second piece, and place it on top. Sara cut bread for each of us before walking back to the icebox, this time returning with a pitcher of milk and sitting it on the table. She gets four glasses and passes one to each of us before taking a seat and making herself a sandwich.

As she lifts it to her mouth, she looks over at Sean and asks, "will they be back tonight?"

Sean already has a mouthful and is filling his glass with milk. He chews quickly and swallows before responding. "I'm not sure. I guess it depends on what they find."

I watch Sara as she nods her head before biting into her sandwich. Her hands tremble while she moves her stare to the ceiling. I feel bad for her. I know she is scared, and Patrick is not here to comfort her. I take a bite of my sandwich and pour myself a glass of milk. It tastes good. A little dry, I think, with the heel, so I wash it down with a big gulp of milk. I really am hungry.

Continuing to eat my sandwich, I watch each of them chew and swallow without saying another word. The dinner table, that is usually full of laughter and joy, has been replaced by a somber setting. The air is warm and stuffy as it is now midday. Sounds of birds chirping, the buzz of automobiles driving, and the hum of men talking are coming in through the open windows that create a peaceful background noise. I am certain we are all thinking about the current situation, but none of us wants to say anything out loud. We are content to eat our sandwiches and pretend nothing is wrong for the moment.

"I'm going to go check on the girl," Sara says as she stands to her feet. Her sandwich is barely eaten.

None of us say anything. We all nod our head in agreement and continue eating. After only a few moments, she reappears from the cellar and closes the door behind her.

"She's still asleep," she says calmly.

Sara collects her plate and dumps it in the trash before placing it in the sink. She then collects the plate of ham and pitcher of milk, returning them to the icebox. Leaving the bread on the table, she walks past me, brushing her hand across my shoulder and trailing it along my back.

"I'm going upstairs to lie down for a bit," she says as she exits the room.

None of us move or acknowledge her statement. We continue eating until all three of us have finished our sandwiches and drank the last of our milk. Each of us stare off in our own direction, content with the peace and quiet. After several minutes, Uncle Jack gets up and walks into the living room, taking his place on the sofa. Sean is the next to get up, so I join him after clearing the plates and glasses.

As I walk into the living room, Sean is busy clipping the tommy guns and moving about, checking to ensure the guns are full of ammunition. I sit down next to Uncle Jack at the far end of the sofa and eventually Sean joins us and takes a seat in a chair off to the side. Each of us holds a weapon but all remain quiet.

We stay like that for the next couple hours, each of us occasionally getting up and using the restroom or walking around the rooms and looking out the windows. None of us speak and seem content to stand guard, just being with one another. Uncle Jack rarely sips his moonshine, and I know it must be difficult for him. For as long as I can remember, he'll get rip-roaring drunk every day and puts on a show for us. Whether it is singing and dancing a jig or telling a whopper story, he always keeps us entertained. Now, he sits grim faced and guarded. He knows, I believe, this will not end well. Each time I go to one of the windows, I notice the men have moved further and further from us but are visibly moving about the neighborhood. I am nervous they will find something and come back to catch us by surprise.

Eventually, Sara comes down the stairs and stops

in the living room. "Any visitors?" she asks calmly.

Sean shakes his head, and she disappears into the kitchen. I hear the cellar door open and the faint sound of her footsteps as she descends the stairs. My ears perk as I hear muffled sounds of conversation, and I get up and walk into the kitchen in time to see Sara come through the door.

"She's hungry and hurting," she states as she walks past me to the icebox.

"Do you need me to do anything?" Asks Sean as I realize he had walked up behind me.

"No," says Sara as she makes a sandwich and pours a glass of water. "I'm going to get her fed and change her bandage."

Sara again disappears downstairs to the cellar before Sean closes the door and files off into the living room. I stay and press my ear close to the door. I cannot hear much, but every once in a while, there are faint voices, and I imagine Sara carefully tending to Emma's wounds while visiting with her. Sara is a loving woman, and I know Emma will see that. For some reason, thinking about that gives me peace and I want it for her. I understand how scared she must be. Hell, both of them are afraid, I worry.

After some time, I hear footsteps coming up the stairs and I move back away from the door. Sara is surprised as she sees me standing there, but still manages a smile as she carries the dishes to the sink. Walking past me, she stops and rubs my arm. While making eye contact with me, she speaks softly, "She's going to be OK."

Sara continues on into the living room and takes my spot at the end of the sofa. I wait around in the kitchen for a minute before finally joining the others in the living room and take a seat on the sofa between Uncle Jack and Sara.

Sara and Sean talk for a minute about how Emma is doing and about what Sara had given her for her wound and to help her sleep. "She needs rest," Sara says. "That's the best thing for her right now."

She leans back, seeming to relax and places her hand on my head, rubbing my hair up and down in a slow motion. "It's good to hear your voice," she says peacefully. "I bet you have a beautiful singing voice."

Sara was always around us back when I talked regularly and our folks were alive, so she remembers. Although, I think to myself, my voice has changed and is deeper. She and Patrick dated for years before getting married and they were always around one another. She grew up just down the road, but both of her parents passed away a few years back from pneumonia. I know she and Patrick always find solace in the fact that they share a bond of having both sets of parents dead at such an early age and rely on one another to keep going.

"Not as good as his ole Uncle Jack, I bet!" The sound cuts through my thoughts as Uncle Jack slaps my leg and has a good laugh.

"I can't sing, and I can't dance," I say while trying to muster a laugh along with the others.

The four of us sat there, laughing and telling stories. I listened a lot more than I spoke, but if asked a question, I would answer. It was mostly nothing but kept us entertained. Occasionally, Sean would get up from his seat and peer out a nearby window or look out the screen door. He always returned to his chair and tried to join in the conversation, but I can tell that he is uneasy. The chatter went on for quite a while before we eventually fell silent and sit quietly staring at the walls.

As dusk falls and nighttime peeks around the corner, we continue the waiting game. At random, we hear the sound of men climbing in their automobiles and leaving the neighborhood. Each time, Sean rises from his seat to stare out the screen door. He constantly keeps a rifle in his hand and appears uneasy. Matter of fact, we all are. The thought of knowing people are looking for a girl we have resting in our cellar is an odd one to get used to. She is right under their nose and if they find out, it will be hell to pay. I don't like sitting here like this. I am ready to fight, and I know who I want most of all.

Uncle Jack is the first to fall asleep. He tried hard not to drink too much and was better than usual, but he succumbed to his addiction. His body slumps with his head resting on the back of the sofa, mouth wide open and snoring loudly. His chest heaves and shakes as he creates a multitude of sounds, ever changing as the noise cuts through our silence. I get up and take a seat on an open chair across the room to escape the obnoxious sounds he is producing.

Sara also rises from the sofa and disappears briefly before returning with a blanket. She puts his shotgun on the floor next to the sofa and covers Uncle Jack from head to toe before casting glances at both Sean and I. "I'm off to bed, myself." She says while holding her stare at Sean.

He nods at her as if to reassure her that everything will be OK and she must have accepted that as she walks past Sean, over to me and, while leaning over, kisses my forehead.

"Goodnight boys," she says. "I'll check on the girl

later tonight, but you may want to peek in at her and see if she's awake here in a bit. If she is, come get me."

"Goodnight," Sean replies.

"Goodnight," I repeat.

As she climbs the stairs, she glances back over her shoulder and smiles at me one more time. I think to myself that it must be odd for her to hear me talk and it will probably take some time to get used to.

Sean stands and walks to the screen door before stepping outside. "Come on Cieran," he says. "Let's get some air."

I follow with my rifle in hand. As I step through the door, I notice nighttime is upon us. A nearly full moon illuminates the surroundings, allowing me to see lanterns all around us and still moving through the bottoms.

Sean pulls a cigarette pack from his pocket and lights it before passing one to me. As I strike my match and place it to the end of my cigarette, a car starts up and pulls to the edge of our driveway before once again cutting the engine off. Through the moonlight, I can see two men inside and both are watching Sean and I.

"Should I hide my gun?" I ask quietly.

Sean inhaled deeply and holds it a moment before finally exhaling. "Nah," he replies nonchalantly. "Let 'em see it." He is staring intently at the men in the car. "Are you OK?" he asks, turning his attention to me.

I don't know exactly what he means. I assume he is worried about my state of mind with all that is going on. "Yeah," I respond. "I'm OK."

He turns and walks next to me, while speaking in almost a whisper he says. "This is gonna get bad. There's no going back on what you did, and we have to get

Bobby for what he did to mom and dad. We're gonna have to take out all of 'em before they find out we have the girl."

I nod my head in agreement. I am ready now. Hell, I think, I was ready yesterday.

"I wanna make sure you understand," he continues. "We're gonna have to do this as a family and be smart about it."

"I'm not scared," I say to him while puffing out my chest. "I wanna kill Bobby Kelley, real bad."

Sean smiles and pats me on the shoulder. "We all do," he says as he flicks his cigarette in the yard. "Tomorrow is gonna be a big day. Let's get some rest, so we're ready."

He opens the screen door and holds it out to let me go in first. Once inside, he closes the main door but doesn't twist the lock. While moving his chair to face the door, he positions a tommy gun on the floor next to it, sits down and places his shotgun across his knees. "I'm gonna be right here," he says. "Will you close and lock the back door on your way to the cellar?"

My ears perk up and my head cocks slightly to the side as I consider the fact that I probably heard him wrong. He looks up at me and gives me a wink. "Think you can keep watch over the girl tonight?"

I nod unconsciously as he continues. "Come get me if she wakes and starts making' a fuss."

As I walk into the kitchen, I can't help but feel proud that Sean trusts me to keep an eye on Emma. This means a lot to me, and I won't let him down. I close all the windows in the kitchen and draw the curtains closed. I twist the lock on the back door to find it already locked. I try the knob twice, anyway. Content that it is locked, I open the cellar door and go downstairs, leaving it open behind me.

The cellar is dimly lit as a single lantern burns at one end and casts dancing shadows along the wall. It is cool down here and smells of dampness. Finding a chair, I pull it alongside the bed and sit down. Emma is nestled up to her neck under the covers. Her arms lay alongside her body on top of the blankets and her nose appears a bit cherry, I think. Her lips are drawn closed and her nostrils flare with each breath. The cellar is deathly quiet, and I can hear her breathing noisily as she sleeps. Not snoring, something different.

I again recognize her beauty as the light bounces off her auburn hair and illuminates her rosy lips. Her light skin tone has returned from the greyness as earlier and I imagine her emerald, green eyes as I had seen them at the hotel. Not wide eyed and afraid as I have seen recently. My stomach churns at the idea that she is laid up in this foreign bed because I hurt her. I hate it and wish I could take it back. While watching her sleep, I feel so much love for her. I never want to see her go. I wonder to myself how I can kill Bobby Kelley and then she can stay with me forever.

Turning my chair to the side, I put my feet up on the edge of the bed and hunker down in the chair, trying to get comfortable. It is quite colder down here than upstairs, and I am getting a chill. I cross my arms in front of me and close my eyes. While leaning my head back, I ponder, how am I going to kill Bobby Kelley...

Chapter 10

The Confrontation

I am jolted out of my sleep by the movement of the bed, and I quickly jump to my feet, unaware of my surroundings. It is dim and I am groggy as I wipe the sleep from my eyes. At first, I don't know where I am but slowly remember while looking around the cellar. I hadn't felt tired when I closed my eyes, but I guess I was wrong. I heard footsteps on the stairs a couple times throughout the night and glanced up to find Sean once and Sara once, each looking in on us. Each time, I quickly fell back to sleep after feeling no worry as they hadn't said anything to me.

As my mind adjusts to the surroundings, I notice Emma wiggling on the bed and once again stares at me wide eyed. I sit back down in the chair for a moment and continue trying to catch my bearings before again standing to my feet.

I walk toward the staircase and peer up into the kitchen. It is fairly dark, with no noise coming from above. I wonder what time it is before walking back to the bed. On a bedside table is a glass of water that I assume Sara had left and reach out to hand it to Emma.

She hesitates for a moment before finally taking the glass. She watches me intently through her now narrowed eyes as she lifts the glass to her lips and takes a drink. It must taste good, I think as she follows up with another large gulp and finishes the entire glass.

Holding the empty glass out to me, she asks, "what time is it?"

"Not sure," I respond. "It looks pretty dark up there." I glance down at the empty glass before asking, "would you like some more?"

Emma blinks a few times before quietly responding, "Yes, please."

I immediately turn and trot up the stairs to the sink. While filling the glass, I push the curtains to the side and see that it is barely past day break. I shut the water off and peek into the living room. Uncle Jack is lying on the couch snoring loudly and I cannot see Sean anywhere in the room. Without another thought, I trot back downstairs and hand the glass to Emma.

This time, she doesn't hesitate as she lifts the glass to her mouth and drinks it down in three large gulps, taking only a moment to breathe between each swallow. After handing me the empty glass, she scoots forward to sit all the way up but winces from the pain as recognizable on her face.

"Would you like some more?" I ask.

She shakes her head no.

I stare at the empty glass, then glance back at Emma. "Are you hurting?"

Emma nods and lowers the blanket. She peels back the gauze and looks at her wound. "Why would you do this to me?" she asks as she lifts her gaze to reach mine.

I am taken aback as I hear the question she asks. Unprepared, I respond quietly. "I didn't mean to."

Emma stares at me intently. Her expression has changed from fear and is now replaced with a quizzical expression, showing that she doesn't understand. She adjusts her body to lie on her side with her elbow resting on the bed, not speaking a word.

After what feels like an eternity, I sheepishly continue. "You scared me, and I reacted. I really didn't mean to."

Emma seems to ease a bit while she moves her gaze from me to look around the room. "Where is the lady?" she asks.

"I think she's still in bed," I reply, thankful to move the conversation forward.

She nods and takes a moment before responding. "I need to visit the washroom."

I sit there for a moment looking at her, then gaze around the room before it finally sinks in that she has to go. Fumbling about and looking completely silly, I scramble up the stairs. "I'll get Sara," I yell back.

As I run through the kitchen and start across the living room floor, I startle Uncle Jack, who is still asleep on the sofa. He struggles to sit up while reaching for the shotgun but cannot find it. The front door is open, and I catch a glimpse of Sean smoking a cigarette while standing on the front porch. As I bound up the staircase, I hear the screen door bounce closed and hear him ask behind me, "What's wrong?"

I don't stop and turn down the hallway, bursting into Sara's room, where she is asleep on the bed. "She has to use the restroom," I blurt out.

Sara is immediately awakened and wrestles with

the blankets as if her life depends on it. With her feet hitting the floor, she looks at me and seems to calm. "What is it?" She asks.

"She has to use the restroom," I repeat.

Sara exhales a sigh of relief and gets up off the bed. While putting on her robe, she replies, "OK. I'll take care of it."

Noticing that I scared her and now feeling uncomfortable, I turn and head back downstairs. Uncle Jack is standing with shotgun in hand, looking at me as I enter the room.

Sean walks back into the living room from the kitchen, joining Uncle Jack and staring at me also. "What's going on?" he asks again, displaying a worrisome expression.

I feel bad as I realize that I have scared everyone while running through the house. They are already on edge, I think, and don't need me pushing them further.

"She has to use the restroom," I answer calmly.

I turn to find Sara coming down the stairs. She pats me on my shoulder and wraps her robe, cinching the belt securely around her. She continues past me, disappearing into the kitchen. "I'll take care of it," she repeats.

I look back at Sean as he watches Sara disappear around the corner before finally turning his gaze to me. He stares at me quizzically for a moment before finally asking, "Everything alright?"

I nod and we all three seem to relax.

"Anything going about?" asks Uncle Jack as he stretches his arms wide.

Sean sighs and moves back to peer out the screen door. "Not really," he responds. "These guys have been here all night."

I follow him to the door and look out. The automobile is still parked across the road at the end of the driveway, and the two men inside appear to be staring at the house. I'm sure it startled them how fast Sean came inside. I worry, and that makes me ashamed of myself for panicking.

"No sign of Dutch?" asks Uncle Jack.

"No, not yet" Replies Sean. "I'm sure everyone will be back soon."

Sean is still staring out the door as I peer past him. I can see dew on the lawn and know the sun hasn't been up for long.

"I'll get some coffee on," Uncle Jack says as he walks into the kitchen.

I watch as Sean stares out the screen door while watching the men out front. He always has a seriousness about him, but this is much more. He is nervous; I think.

"Any idea when Patrick is getting back?" Uncle Jack asks from the next room.

I hear the water come on while Sean answers. "No idea."

"What's that, lad?" Uncle Jack asks, shutting the water flow off.

"I don't know," Sean repeats, just a little louder. "It depends on if he has a meeting this morning. Long way back from Kansas City."

Uncle Jack walks back into the living room. "We need to get this thing settled," he says as he picks up his jug of whisky. He pulls the cork out of it and peers in with one eye closed. "Boy," he says aloud. "Fetch Uncle Jack a jar of shine from the shed, would ya?"

I know immediately that he is talking to me. I

start through the kitchen and out the back door. As I descend the stairs, I see another car with two men parked out back in Crow's yard and near our property line. Stopping in my tracks, I stare at them, and they stare back. They make me uncomfortable, yet I continue toward the shed and disappear inside.

I realize how protected the Kelleys' are. They think of everything; I feel. It will be tough to get the best of them. I rip back the tarp covering our stash of moonshine, and I am bewildered at how much we have accumulated. Since Uncle Jack has increased our production, we stockpiled it. There were barrels stacked to the ceiling and case after case filled with jugs of moonshine. Our delivery truck was loaded to the brim and tarped also. We have just about everything a man can want. Brandy, whisky, sour mash, you name it, and we have it. Patrick wants to expand past Dutch's operation, and we are ready. When we kill the Kelleys', I think, we can take over and be the biggest in the county.

I reach inside an open case closest to me and pull out a jar. Without putting the tarp back, I go outside and close the door behind me. Again, as I cross the yard to the back porch, I stare at the men in the car, and they still stare back. I grit my teeth and scowl at them, but I'm not sure they notice as I am moving fast.

Once inside, I close the door behind me and turn to find both Uncle Jack and Sean standing in the kitchen. They had been speaking but quieted as soon as I entered. I stare at them for a moment before handing the jar to Uncle Jack. He looks like the cat that swallowed the chicken; I think to myself and glare at him, letting him know that I know they were talking about me.

Uncle Jack doesn't seem to notice and thanks me as he takes the jug from me. He pours a cup of coffee for himself, adding a shot of moonshine from the jug. As he pours a cup for Sean, he lifts the jug out toward him.

"No," Sean says while shaking his head. "It's a little too early for all of that."

"Suit yourself," Uncle Jack replies as he passes a cup to Sean. He leans back against the counter and lifts his cup to his mouth, sips loudly before shaking his head at nothing. "How long before the Kelleys' come back?"

Sean lifts his cup to his lips and blows on it but does not take a drink. "Not long," he says. "I wouldn't rest if my daughter was missing."

Uncle Jack nods in agreement and takes another sip of his coffee. His head turns to watch as Sara opens the cellar door with a bedpan in hand. All of us watch as she struggles to close the door behind her while keeping the pan steady.

"How is she?" asks Sean.

As she walked to the back door, she replies. "Better."

While twisting the knob on the back door, I open my mouth to tell her there are men out there, but Sean is ahead of me. "There are guys out there," he says.

Sara stops and stands for a moment, looking at the door. She turns and walks to the sink, dumps the pan and turns on the water. Uncle Jack appears disgusted and snorts at her.

"Warn a man, why don't ya!" he cries out.

Sara seems unamused as she rinses the pan and shakes it dry. "What time is it?" she asks.

"Quarter after seven," Sean replies as he finally lifts the coffee cup to his lips and sips gently.

Sara lays the bedpan on the floor before washing her hands. "She's hungry, so I'm gonna make her some breakfast. Anyone else want anything?" she asks.

Both Uncle Jack and Sean shake their heads, and I keep quiet. Without acknowledging me, Sara pulls out a skillet and cracks some eggs. The skillet sizzles as she adds the eggs and I can immediately smell the eggs frying, making me hungry. She walks to the icebox and pulls out a couple of pieces of ham. While adding them to the skillet, she asks nonchalantly, "what now, Sean?"

He seems to expect her question as he takes another sip of the coffee. "I don't know," he replies. "Dutch will be back soon, and I hope Patrick returns before then. Not going to be able to hold them off forever."

Sara nods as she continues cooking the eggs and ham. She walks past me and pulls a plate out of the cabinet, sitting it on the counter next to her. "I changed her bandages and doctored the wound," she says. "She's much better today, but still in a lot of pain."

I watch as Sara works to cook breakfast for her houseguest. Her face is drawn and is noticeably nervous while turning the ham over. Her hands shake wildly and there seems to be a difference in her tone. "I'd like to give her a proper bath if we can," she continues. "It's the right thing to do."

Sean again sips his coffee but doesn't look at Sara. He also seems a little more nervous this morning. He finally nods his head in agreement, but neither looks up at one another and I wonder if she sees him.

Sara covers the fire on the stove and slides the pan to the side. She picks up the plate and adds the ham, then the eggs. She walks over to me and hands me the plate.

"Take this to her, please," she asks politely.

I nod as I take the plate from her and walk to the counter to get a fork.

"Take her some of that milk, please. It'll be good for her."

I turn to look at Sara, but she is already walking around the corner into the living room. Both Uncle Jack and Sean still stand in the kitchen sipping their coffee, but neither look at me.

Sitting the plate down on the counter, I pour a glass of milk. As I walk to the cellar door, I glance back at them to find they are still standing next to each other, holding their cup of coffee and staring at the floor. I can't help but worry about them all, but I let it go and continue on with my task.

As I enter the cellar, my footsteps interrupt Emma while she is feeling around her wound. Startled, she quickly pulls the blankets over her and folds her hands in front of her, resting on her lap. Sara had gotten an extra blanket and folded it up behind her with a couple of pillows, allowing her to halfway sit up. I hand the plate to her and sit the glass of milk on the bedside table.

"Do you need anything else?" I ask, trying to be helpful.

Emma lifts the fork and pokes at the eggs to bust the yolk. "Sit down," she replies. "I don't want to be alone."

I pull the chair close to the bed facing toward her and sit down.

"When can I go home?" she asks while lifting a bite of eggs to her mouth.

Swallowing the lump in my throat, I respond without an actual answer. "Don't know. Maybe soon, I think."

She nods while chewing and stares at the food on her plate. "I remember you," she says. "You were at the hotel."

I nod at her but remain quiet. I am very uncomfortable sitting here and carrying on a conversation with her. I don't have any practice with this.

"Why did you come to my house?" she asks.

"To see you," I reply, while shifting in my chair nervously.

Emma lifts her head and stares at me suspiciously. "Why would you do that?"

Again, I swallow the lump in my throat that doesn't seem to go away. "I thought you were beautiful," I admit. "I just wanted to see you again."

Her cheeks turn red, and she allowed a slight smile to cross her face, melting my heart immediately. "I never meant to hurt you," I continue. "It just happened. It was an accident."

She takes another bite, and I lower my head, fidgeting with my trouser legs as I wipe my sweaty hands. "I think I love you," I mumble.

As the words slip from my mouth, I can feel my cheeks warm, and I lift my head to make eye contact.

Emma again smiles and chuckles a bit. "You have an odd way of showing it," she says.

I sort of laugh also and squirm in my chair while feeling the awkwardness between the two of us.

"My head hurts," she says as she lays the fork on her plate before lifting her hand to the back of her head and rubbing it through her hair. "I have a knot and scab right here."

Again, I look down and rub on my trouser legs. "I did that too," I reply sheepishly. "I dropped you and you hit your head on the ground."

She takes a drink of milk before taking another bite. Chewing slowly, she looks confused while asking, "Why did you kidnap me?"

"I don't know," I admit. "I didn't mean to hurt you and just took you with me when I left." I lift my head to look at her in hopes she sees I am sincere. "I wish I could take it all back."

Emma continues to chew but keeps her head down, staring at her plate. "I wanna go home," she mutters softly and sounds as if she might cry.

I don't respond because I don't know what to say. I just sit there for a few moments watching her. I don't want her to go. I know what I have to do to her father, and I don't want to give her back. I want to keep her forever.

Sean's voice rings out from upstairs. "Cieran!" He yells. "Get up here."

I immediately jump to my feet and climb up the stairs, thankful to get away from her line of questioning. As I near the top, I hear Emma speak out from below. "Cieran? That's your name."

I don't stop, only slow a bit as I close the cellar door behind me before entering the living room. Sean is standing at the screen door with Uncle Jack behind him but slightly off to the side.

"They're here," he says while continuing to look out the door.

As I peek around Sean and stare out the screen door, I watch as Dutch and Bobby Kelley get out of their car. They are joined in the road by the men that sat watch all night in the car parked outside, and I realize now that one man is Evan Blake. A third car pulls up behind Dutch's and out steps Captain Lewis. All five of them stand in a circle in the middle of the road, speaking to one another just out of earshot. Occasionally, Dutch or Bobby, or both, turn to look toward our house before returning their gaze back to someone speaking.

Uncle Jack walks calmly over to the sofa and picks up his shotgun. He takes position off to the side and out of sight as he clenches his weapon tightly. I immediately follow suit and pick up my rifle, finding the same spot where I can see out onto the porch. I watch as Sean adjusts the pistol tucked in his trousers before stepping out onto the porch moments before Dutch climbs the steps.

"Dutch." He says while nodding his head in Dutch's direction.

Dutch continues up the stairs and stops directly in front of Sean before responding. He is breathing heavily and nods back at him. "Hello, Sean." he replies. "I see Patrick has yet to return."

"No," Sean states in agreement. "And I don't know when to expect him."

"That's alright," Dutch says. "I'll find out when he gets home, and I will return." His cold black eyes are staring intently at Sean, and he stands far too close for comfort. Evan Blake and the other gentleman from the car had joined Dutch, standing just off the steps. They are watching closely and seem poised to pounce at any moment. Captain Lewis and Bobby are still talking in the middle of the road, and I watch them for a while as Bobby's hands are flailing around while his body lurches forward. I know he is clearly yelling and most likely getting onto Captain Lewis.

"Any word on your granddaughter?" Sean asks in an attempt to relax the tension.

Dutch crosses his hands in front of him. "Now Sean, if I had, do you think I'd be standing on your porch this morning?" He hesitates a moment before continuing. "It's as if she has disappeared."

He pats Sean on the arm and narrows his stare. "Don't worry though, my boy," he says sharply. "They are gonna question every person in this shithole neighborhood today and if they know anything, I'm sure they'll be willing to share it." His thick Irish accent seems more prevalent today, and I wonder if the stress he is under caused it.

"I already told you we don't know anything," Sean responds assertively.

"Aye, I know ya did." Dutch says, while scowling even more. "All of ya's are gonna have to answer some questions from Captain Lewis and Evan. Seems a little odd for everything that happened next door, yet none of you know anything. Don't ya think?"

"Like I said…"

"Yeah, yeah," Dutch says, cutting Sean off while waving his hand at him as if he doesn't matter. "You weren't here. Story checks out, but they were."

He now points toward the house, and I can see him staring directly at me. There isn't an ounce of fear in his eyes, as I know he can see my rifle.

"I will find out what happened to my granddaughter," he continues. "Or I will kill every son of a bitch in this county."

Dutch turns and walks back down the steps. "That much you can count on." He calls back while passing by Evan before joining Bobby and Captain Lewis on the road.

Evan Blake stands at the edge of the steps for a moment while locking eyes with Sean. Neither speaking a word, nor blinking. Seeming to size each other up and intimidate the other, I wonder. Evan hasn't worked for Dutch very long and Sean doesn't know who he is. He just met him yesterday, but I guess that wasn't really a formal introduction. It is a long uncomfortable silence before Evan finally speaks. "Gonna speak with your neighbors first," he says confidently. "Then we'll be back here, probably be a couple of hours."

"We'll be here," Sean responds briskly, standing his ground.

"Oh, I'm counting on that," he replies as he turns and nonchalantly walks to the road, joining the others.

Sean remains on the porch and lights a cigarette as he watches the men talk for a few more minutes. I watch as Dutch and Bobby, walk back to their car and can't help but notice how Bobby's face is red and appears full of fear. He is probably thinking the worst for Emma; I wonder. Dutch is not afraid, though. As he opens the door, he glances back toward the house, watching Sean. His hollow eyes narrow and nostrils flare while he stands locked in eye contact with him. He yells something back to Evan before finally sitting down and closing the door behind him. Their car turns into our driveway and backs out, taking off in the direction they came and most likely headed back into town.

Evan, Captain Lewis, and the third man have to move as Dutch's car almost backs into them on the way out of the driveway. The three of them stand there pointing and talking for a long time, each occasionally glancing back toward Sean standing on the porch. Eventually, they all three get into Captain Lewis' car and pull away, out of my sight.

Sean stands on the porch for quite a while, staring down the road before finally walking back inside. "Come on Patrick," I hear him mutter to himself. "Get your ass home."

Uncle Jack lays his shotgun on the sofa and picks up a jar of moonshine. I watch as his hand shakes profusely while taking a drink. He wipes his mouth, then lifts it once again to his lips. "It's not good," he says, clearly afraid.

Sean walks over to him and pats him on the shoulder before taking the jar from him. "No, it's not," he says while lifting the jar and gulping down a large drink.

"What are we going to do?"

I turn to see Sara standing at the top of the stairs. She has gotten dressed, but her hair still looks mussed, and I wonder how long she has been standing there.

After taking another drink, Sean replies directly to her. "Have a little while till they come back to talk to you two," he says. "You're gonna have to make them think you don't know anything."

Sara descends the stairs and stands next to me. "I don't know if I can do that," she says softly. "I'm not a good liar."

Sean puts the lid on the jar before sitting it back down on the table. "You're not really lying if you say you didn't see anything that night," he replies, trying to coach her. "Just have to sell them on us not knowing anything until Patrick gets home."

"Then what?" she asks while taking a step toward

Sean. "What're we gonna do when Patrick gets home?"

"Don't know yet," he admits. "All I do know is we can't do anything with them by ourselves."

Sara nods, seeming to accept the unsatisfying words Sean speaks. "What about him?" she asks while pointing toward me.

"They're not gonna ask him anything," Sean says while trying to comfort her. "Nobody but us knows he can even talk."

Sara nods again before covering her face with her hands as she starts weeping. Uncle Jack walks across the room and hugs her tightly. I can see the fear in his eyes as well as he passes in front of me.

"It's gonna be OK, Sara," Sean says, speaking softly. "We'll be OK."

I know no one in the room believes that. We have the granddaughter of one of the most powerful families around the area in our cellar and she is hurt by my hand. I feel guilt take over my body while watching Uncle Jack hold Sara as she cries. Sean, although steady, is certainly nervous as he works diligently to be the rock for our family.

I walk to the piano and sit my rifle on the bench. I grab an unopened pack of cigarettes off the back and walk outside. I can feel them watching me as I sit down in the rocker and fish in my pocket for the matches. I hate how much trouble I've brought on the people I love. I got Crow killed, hurt Emma, and most likely this is going to end with others' hurt. I light my cigarette and rock my chair violently as I try to think. I can hear them return to conversation about what they're going to say when Evan and Captain Lewis return. They are rehearsing and Sean is leading them and correcting them as they go.

My mind races while sitting there, listening to the three of them work out their plan. I watch as men move about through our neighbors' yards and cars are passing more frequently than usual. I can see down the road and off to the right, Captain Lewis' car is in the driveway of one of our friends. They are also moonshiners, and we have a good relationship with them, but you never know with people. I wonder how many people saw me riding back to Crow's house on that horse and how long it will take for one of them to break. What will Dutch do to my family if someone recognized me and tells them?

As I consider many outcomes, I can feel the anxiety well up inside of me. I lift my hands out in front and gaze at them. Steady, I think to myself. Not a tremble nor a shake, and I know what I need to do. I need to kill Bobby Kelley and tell Dutch what happened. I know he loved my father and if he finds out what Bobby did, then maybe he will forgive us and let everyone live. He can have his granddaughter back and all will be whole.

I stay there for a while longer, imagining ways for me to sneak up on Bobby and kill him. I can picture Dutch's face as he forgives me for killing his son under the circumstances. The sunlight is beaming, birds chirping off in the distance, and a slight breeze makes this day feel perfect to me.

Content with my plan, I rise from the rocker and go back inside. All three of them stand silent as I walk past them, climb up the stairs and slip into my room. From my drawer, I fish out my bone-handled knife that Crow had given me. I slide it into the sheath made of leather and brightly colored beads and put it on a belt. I place the belt around my hips and cinch it tight.

Walking across the living room, I again feel all eyes in the room on me, but now they have stopped speaking. As I enter the kitchen, I try to figure out how I am going to get my guns and satchel out of the house without any of them catching me. I'll figure it out, I think as I open the door to the cellar. I just want to see Emma once more and then I'll figure a way out of here to go and kill her father.

As I enter the cellar, I can feel my heartbeat pick up. I am calm but energized by my newfound mission. Emma is still partially sitting up but appears to be trying to sleep. She opens her eyes and turns to face me as I take a seat on the chair next to the bed.

"Hello Cieran," she mutters, clearly tired.

"Hello Emma," I reply. "Are you feeling, OK?"

She sighs and shakes her head no. "I'm hurting and have a headache."

"I'll see if Sara has any more pain medicine," I say, while taking her hand in mine. She pulls back a little and stares at me, bewildered. I grip her hand tighter and feel the anxiety grow within me and I forget what I came here to say. "I'm leaving for a little while to take care of some things. When I come back, we can be together and maybe get married."

Emma's face tightens and again she tries to pull her hand from mine. "We just need to get you healed up so you're better," I say softly. "Get some rest and I'll see you soon."

She pulls her hand back again and this time I let go before standing to my feet. "I don't understand," she says while clearly looking horrified.

I brush my hand through her hair and lean down

to kiss her forehead. Emma flinches and turns her head away from me, so I pull back and rub her cheek. "I'll explain everything when I get home," I say as I take a step back, away from the bed.

Emma's expression is that of pure astonishment, and I stand there staring at her for a second, trying to understand why. She doesn't understand; I worry. She will see when I get back to explain everything to her, I believe. I give her a quick smile and turn before bounding up the stairs and walking out into the kitchen. As I close the cellar door, I come face to face with Sean.

"What do you think you're doing?" he asks directly.

Surprised, I jump backward and stare at him stone faced, prepared to lie.

Sean is watching me intently but breathing heavily. "Don't even think about leaving this house," he says sternly while reaching out for my arm.

I am about to respond as I hear Uncle Jack yell out from the other room. "Pat's home!"

Sean glares at me for another moment before finally walking into the living room toward the screen door. I think about ducking out the kitchen door, but my satchel and guns are in the living room. I wish I had brought them with me as now I'm stuck, and I do not know what to do.

I hesitantly relent and follow Sean into the living room and stand with him, staring out the screen door. Patrick and Ryan step out of the car almost simultaneously, with Patrick looking over his shoulder at the car parked across the road. Ryan stretches his arms to the sky and arches his back while waiting on Patrick, seeming not to notice anything. As Patrick climbs the stairs and opens the screen door, he takes one last look back before stepping inside.

"Whose car is that?" he asks.

He stops just inside the door, with Ryan standing directly behind him, holding the screen door open. Patrick turns his attention inside. He first looks at Sean, then me, then toward Uncle Jack and ending with Sara. "Whose car is that?" he asks again. He doesn't wait for an answer as he sees the expression on Sara's face. He quickly follows with another question and appears worried. "What's wrong?"

Patrick walks past Sean, surveying the room and notices the guns laying out in the open. Sara begins to cry and covers her face with her hands. He walks directly over to her and wraps his arms around her before turning to face Sean. The screen door slams shut as Ryan enters and stops just inside the door as he also feels the tension inside.

"Something's happened," Sean finally replies. "It's a bad deal."

Patrick holds Sara with one arm as he stares at Sean through narrowed eyes and a serious demeanor. "Go on," he says. "What is it?"

Uncle Jack takes a seat on the sofa and Ryan follows without speaking, sitting at the opposite end also staring intently at Sean as he realizes something is wrong. I moved from the door to allow room for Patrick to enter and I am now standing near the kitchen, across the room. All eyes are on Sean, and you can cut the tension with a knife.

Sean takes a deep breath. "Cieran went to Dutch's house to see a girl," he begins.

For a brief second, Patrick turns to look at me but

quickly returns his attention to Sean as he continues to tell my story. I am relieved to hear Sean tell it as he is keeping mostly to the facts and repeats it closely to the way I had told him. All the color leaves Patrick's face as Sean describes how Bobby Kelley killed our parents. He stands there holding Sara and listens intently. His facial expression changes with each emotion and seems to cringe while Sean describes Crow's death. I glance at Ryan a few times throughout the story. His attention fixed on Sean also, but his expression never wavers. I can see the anger in his face as he grits his teeth and clenches his jaw, but he too remains quiet throughout the entire story.

"The girl is in the cellar," Sean says while finishing up.

Patrick immediately lets go of Sara and crosses the floor, stopping to face me as he nears the kitchen. He peers into my eyes and raises his hand to my cheek, rubbing my jawline with his thumb, and I feel the love that he has for me. This lasts only a second as he turns and walks into the kitchen before going down the cellar stairs.

Almost as quickly as he disappeared, he returns to the living room, coming to a stop in the center of the room. "They're going to want blood," he says while making eye contact with each of us.

All at once, Ryan jumps to his feet and yells out, "Let's get 'em! They can't get away with this!"

Patrick crosses the room and hugs him while Uncle Jack pats his leg. "We will get Bobby," he says reassuringly. "But we have to be smart about it. Dutch is too strong and has too many men." He steps back but keeps one arm on Ryan's shoulder. "Plus, he has the police on his side."

Ryan isn't satisfied and doesn't seem comforted by Patrick's words. "We have to get them!" he shrieks.

"Dutch has already been here today and said he's coming back," Sean interjects. "Says he wants his bodyguard and Captain Lewis to talk to Uncle Jack and Sara."

Patrick nods as he looks first to Uncle Jack and then to Sara. "I'll make sure they don't speak to you guys," he replies confidently.

"Should be back anytime," Sean adds, trying to keep Patrick up to date.

"OK," replies Patrick as he is noticeably on edge and senses the danger. "Ryan, go out and get our guns and ammo out of the car."

Ryan stands there looking at Patrick with his teeth still gritted and jaw clenched. "I can't believe you don't want to get them," he spurts angrily. "We should kill them all."

Again, Patrick places his arm on Ryan's shoulder. "We will," he replies. "We just have to be ready."

Jerking his shoulder from under Patrick's hand, Ryan stomps across the room and out the screen door. I peek out the window in time to see him open the back door of the car.

"Jack, are you able to speak with Captain Lewis?" Patrick asks, turning his attention away from Ryan.

Uncle Jack glances up at Patrick and then back down at the jar of moonshine on the table. He picks it up and opens the lid slowly. He lifts it to his mouth but replies before taking a drink. "An ole drunk has no fear."

Patrick smiles as Uncle Jack takes a swallow before putting the jar back on the table. "I think you're right," he says proudly.

The sound of a gunshot rings throughout the house and causes all of us to jump. Someone yells off in the distance, followed by another gunshot, and then another.

"Ryan!" yells Sean as he bursts through the screen door and takes off across the porch.

Chapter 11

The War

Patrick grabs the shotgun off the table next to Uncle Jack and fishes a pistol from the back of his trousers as he runs out the door behind Sean. I run across the room and grab my pistol, stuffing it in my trouser pocket before picking up my rifle. I am only a few steps behind as I pass through the screen door and down the stairs. Just as I reach the road, I watch about a block down as a man lifts his gun and fires three shots at Ryan. I stop in my tracks when I see Ryan fall to the ground and start crawling backward.

Sean is firing shots as he sprints down the road with Patrick not far behind. I can see three men running for cover as Patrick joins him and is now shooting at them as well. All three men find cover behind trees while Sean kneels down and picks up Ryan. Patrick is still firing as Sean runs back toward the house, carrying Ryan in his arms. I kneel down on one knee and take aim at one of the men as they step out from behind the tree as he aims his pistol toward Sean. I pull the trigger and hit the man square in the neck, dropping him instantly. I'm not sure who he is, but I hope it is Evan Blake, I think. I do not like him.

I am taking aim at another one of the men as Sean sprints past me, with Patrick close behind. "Come on," Patrick yells as he grabs my arm and jerks me to my feet, pulling me toward the house.

Sara screams from inside the house as Patrick drags me across the porch and into the doorway. I stumble and fall as Sean lays Ryan's body in the middle of the floor.

"Is he OK?" Patrick yells back at Sean while taking position just inside the screen door and aiming his shotgun down the road.

Sean doesn't respond. He rips Ryan's shirt open, exposing his bloody torso with two open wounds. One near the center of his stomach and the second on his right chest, just below the nipple. Blood seeps from the wound as Ryan wheezes and coughs blood into the air.

Patrick moves past them to grab a box of shells and glances down at Ryan's wounds. "Dammit, Ryan!" he shouts.

Sara joins Sean with a handful of rags and kneels beside him, wiping the blood as it continues to flow from Ryan's body. She is crying pitifully as Sean takes the rags and places them over the wounds, applying pressure. I join them and also kneel by his side to only stare as I watch them work. Ryan is writhing on the floor and gasping for air. His legs are kicking in all directions, as if he is searching for a foothold.

Patrick runs back to the door and stares outside as he reloads his shotgun. "Tell me what's going on!" he yells out.

Sean still cannot respond as he holds pressure on the wounds, but Ryan's movement begins to slow. He sits there holding the rags over the bullet holes and stares into Ryan's eyes. I can see his eyes are open and he is staring back at Sean. His chest heaves as he searches for breath. While choking on blood, he asks softly, "Did I get 'em?"

Letting go of one of the rags, Sean runs his hand through Ryan's hair, doing his best to comfort him. "Yeah, you got 'em," he replies while smiling widely. "They didn't even know what hit 'em."

Ryan smiles as he gulps at air a couple of times before his legs fall limp. His lifeless body lays still as blood continues to fall from the corner of his mouth before rolling off of his chin and dripping to the floor. Sean drops his head, and his arms fall loosely to his side while Sara sobs loudly.

Patrick looks back and again asks, "What's going on?"

Sean never lifts his head, only replies somberly, "he's gone."

"Dammit, Ryan," Patrick repeats upon hearing the words. "I told you to wait."

I can hear the sadness in his voice and feel the same myself as I gaze at Ryan's soulless face. Patrick continues watching out the screen door, looking back toward Ryan only once. I stay there looking at his limp body lying lifeless and feel the sadness of his death wash over me. For the second time in as many days, I watch a loved one pass away because of my decisions. This is unacceptable, and I am filled with guilt.

Sean stands to his feet and walks to the couch, retrieving the blanket Uncle Jack had slept with the night before. He causally walks back over and covers Ryan's body while kneeling at his side.

"Here they come," Patrick calls out. "Sara, go to the cellar and wait for me there."

Still crying, Sara jumps to her feet and disappears into the kitchen. I can hear the cellar door close and the faint scurrying of her feet down the steps. Uncle Jack stands and points his shotgun at the window. Tears stain his rosy cheeks and his hands are shaking uncontrollably, causing the barrel of the shotgun to vibrate. He ducks and stands up straight over and over, trying to catch a glimpse through the window as to what is going on outside.

"Patrick," a voice I recognize as Captain Lewis' calls out from the road. "You all come out now. We are surrounding you."

Patrick never hesitates and responds quickly by yelling back, "Get Dutch out here and we'll talk."

"Dutch'll be here," he replies. "But I need ya'll to come out with your hands up."

Patrick grits his teeth and takes aim toward the road. "No chance Captain. You killed my brother!" he yells back.

There is a moment of silence before Captain Lewis eventually responds. "Didn't have a choice," he says. "The boy fired on us. I am the law around here."

I stand and jog into the kitchen, peering out each window as I pass. Sure enough, men are positioning themselves all around, ducking behind whatever they can find for cover. At each window throughout the house, I watch as a new car approaches and one or more men get out and take aim at our house. Some are police and some are just suited men I know who work for Dutch. As I reenter the living room, I see Sean is still kneeling at Ryan's side. His head is down, and he appears to be in prayer.

"Come on Patrick," Captain Lewis continues. "It doesn't have to be like this."

As I walk up behind Patrick, I can hear him breathing heavily. I'm not sure if it is because of the situation, we are in or if he is still out of breath from running. He glances at me out of the corner of his eye and reaches his hand back, placing it on my chest as if he is telling me to stay back. I stay and peek out to the road in front of our house. Captain Lewis and Evan Blake are positioned behind their car parked out front. A couple of other cars have joined alongside them and have men leaning over hoods and hiding behind trees. All are pointing guns at our house, and all look ready to fire.

"Get me Dutch," Patrick yells back at him and not budging.

"He's coming, I'm sure of it." Captain Lewis responds. "You killed one of my men, and I need you to come out."

To my surprise, Patrick pushes out the screen door open and steps out onto the porch with shotgun in hand. "You can come up, Lewis," he yells back. "I'll tell you what's going on."

I step into the doorway and grip my rifle tight as I watch Captain Lewis and Evan Blake talk to one another. All the other men take aim at Patrick, and I can sense their unrest as they watch him closely.

After a few moments of quiet, Captain Lewis finally responds. "I ain't coming up there."

"We ain't got no quarrel with you," Patrick replies. "We don't want no more trouble."

Evan Blake whispers something to him and

Captain Lewis shakes his head and talks back to him. They go back and forth for a minute, and I do not know what they might be talking about. Eventually, Captain Lewis yells back at Patrick. "Do I have your word you ain't gonna shoot?"

Patrick takes his finger off the trigger and clutches the shotgun under his arm as he fishes a pack of cigarettes out of his pocket before lighting one. He inhales deeply and pulls it from his lips. "We ain't gonna shoot you Lewis," he says calmly. "You're a lawman, and I just want to explain what's going on. We can fix this."

Hesitantly, Captain Lewis walks around the vehicle and starts up the driveway toward the porch. He points his pistol toward Patrick as he walks, and I am certain that I can see it shaking. His steps are slow and cautious as he makes his way closer. "Why'd that boy shoot at us?" he asks as he stops just a few feet from the porch stairs.

"He's mad is all," Patrick replies nonchalantly. "You see, this ain't just a simple case and I'm gonna need Dutch here before we can sort it all out."

"You can tell me," Captain Lewis says, while trying to gain his confidence. "I am the law around here."

"That you are," Patrick agrees in nodding his head. "But you work for them, so there ain't no use talking to two folks when I need the one pulling the string."

My attention is turned behind me as I hear a clicking noise and watch as Sean puts a magazine in one of the tommy guns. He wears a fierce expression across his face as he chambers a round using his blood-stained hands. He studies the gun, looking it up and down, turning it over and inspecting the bottom.

"You're all going to jail," Captain Lewis replies, seeming to find his courage. "Does this have something to do with the girl?"

I turn back toward the door and watched as Patrick inhales one last time before flicking the cigarette out into the yard. Evan Blake walks around the car and starts toward the porch. The gun he holds rests at his side, and he takes long, purposeful strides as he comes to a stop next to Captain Lewis.

"Where's the girl?" Evan asks bravely.

Captain Lewis jumps a little when he hears Evan speak. He turns his head toward Evan but keeps the gun pointed at Patrick.

"I want to see Dutch," Patrick responds. "Get him here and we'll talk."

"I'm the one you're gonna deal with right now," Evan says forcefully. "Now where's the girl?"

His voice raises, and his face is stern. Unlike Captain Lewis, Evan is steady and appears unbothered by Patrick. He looks calm as he towers over Captain Lewis. The gun resting at his side glimmers in the sunlight and appears as if it is an extension of his body.

As I continue to watch them, I feel my body abruptly pushed to the side as Sean steps through the door and out onto the porch. He holds the tommy gun in his left hand, hanging loosely, and pointed at the ground. Stopping at the steps, he looks directly at Evan before asking. "You the one that killed my brother?"

Evan smiles widely and smirks at Sean, unfazed by his presence and seeming to be amused by it. "That's right," he answers coldly.

Sean nods once before striding down the steps while simultaneously pulling the pistol from the back of his trousers. Evan takes a half step backward and continues smiling as Sean lifts his pistol, shooting Evan directly in his left eye. Evan appears to still be smiling as he drops to his knees with his arm still at his side. Sean fired a second shot straight through Evan's forehead. The action is fast and his head lurches backward, but Evan stays on his knees for a moment before falling forward. Sean has to step sideways to prevent him from falling on his feet.

Captain Lewis screams and jumps backward onto his bottom. He crawls along the driveway as the shots ring out from all around us. He is screaming something as he crawls and eventually reaches his feet toward the end of the driveway before taking refuge behind his car.

Sean's body twists backward as a bullet strikes him. He cries out in anguish while lifting the tommy gun and points it outward. The sound is deafening as he cuts loose and sprays bullets left to right toward anything within range. Bodies fall as others dive for cover while he fires relentlessly.

Patrick fires shot after shot as he moves down the steps toward Sean. I kick the door open and take aim to my left as a man steps out from his hiding spot, drawing down on Sean. As he raises his pistol, I fire and strike the man square in his chest. Blood sprays from his body as he falls backward.

"Kill the bastards!" Uncle Jack yells as he fires a shot, pumps the shotgun and fires again. For the first time in my life, I watch Uncle Jack yell angrily through gritted teeth as he continuously pumps his shotgun and fires out the window.

I turn my attention back outside to see Patrick standing next to Sean as he continues to fire his weapon. Patrick has his shotgun pointed forward and is firing steadily at his target, hitting one man standing close to Captain Lewis' car. Blood splatters through the air as the man falls to the ground and stops moving. I look back to my left toward the man I had just shot in time to catch a glimpse of a man running around the side of the house and once again drawing down on Sean. Sean is not paying attention and is firing the tommy gun in the other direction, not able to see the man. I sling my rifle toward him and inhale calmly while squeezing the trigger. The man is clenching his jaw with teeth showing as he raises his gun to take aim. My bullet hits him in the neck, causing him to fall to the ground. Spurting blood and writhing on the ground, he grips his neck while I fire a second shot, striking him in the chest and bringing his entire body to rest.

As Sean's gun clicks empty of bullets, a second man rounds the left corner of the house. Before he can even lift his gun, I fire and hit him square in the chest. His momentum carries him forward, and he slumps on his side, barely moving.

The gunfire ceases for a moment as Patrick yells out and grabs Sean by the arm. "Get inside."

He has Sean by the arm and is dragging him up the stairs when I catch a glimpse of a man coming around the right side of the house. I turn my body as Patrick lifts his shotgun and fires, hitting the man in the chest. The man's body churns backward, blood sprays the air and his head hits the ground before his feet. I hear the thud as he collapses to the ground and lay motionless.

As Sean and Patrick run through the door, I follow, and we all collapse to the floor as a hail of gunfire burst through our house from all sides. Glass shatters from windows and dust flies as bullets strike walls.

"Get down!" Patrick yells while crawling across the floor toward the ammunition box.

I turn and crawl on my belly toward Sean. While glancing back, I see Uncle Jack start to run. His face writhes in pain as the first shot strikes him in the lower back. He drops his shotgun and falls forward when the second bullet enters the middle of his back. As he falls over the table, he reaches back over his shoulder to feel the wound, but his arm can't reach, allowing him to hit the floor unbraced. Even through the gunfire, I can hear his shriek and the sound of his body as it falls ungracefully with a boom. He's not trying to cover up, just rolls to his back with his feet flat on the floor and knees facing the ceiling. I crawl over to him and hold him tight while I try to shield both of our faces from falling debris.

The gunfire lasts for several minutes but eventually trails off as random shots continually ring out. The last few shots were not even close to us, but I still covered mine and Uncle Jack's face following each burst.

"Hold your fire," someone calls out from outside.

Two, maybe three more shots strike through the house before silence falls. Uncle Jack, writhing with pain, groans and squirms on the floor. I lift my head to look at him and see his eyes are closed and he is grinding his teeth, creating a horrible noise that sends chills down my spine.

"Jack!" Patrick mutters as he slides on his belly

toward us before lifting himself to his knees. "Let me see how bad it is?"

Sean is kneeling next to one box off to the side and has gotten another magazine. I watch as blood runs down his arm and drips to the floor while he locks it into place on the tommy gun. He is shot in the left shoulder but he shows no emotion while working to reload the gun, even as blood continues flowing down his arm. Patrick rolls Uncle Jack to his side. His shirt is soaked in blood and continues to flow as Patrick unbuckles the straps on his overalls and slides them down. After lifting his shirt, Uncle Jack asks quietly, "is it bad?"

Blood is pouring from the two large holes in Uncle Jack's back. Patrick lowers his shirt and rolls Uncle Jack back over. Looking him in the eyes, Patrick answers honestly, "It's bad, Jack."

Uncle Jack begins to cough and blood sprays out of his lips each time with a pool forming on the corner of his mouth. "I knew it," he says and chuckles. Each time he laughs, he coughs and agonizes in pain.

Patrick grabs my arm, pulling me close to him. "Go get Sara," he says before moving back toward Sean.

I bear crawl across the floor to the kitchen before standing upright and running down to the cellar. Sara is on the bed with Emma, and they are holding each other tightly, both crying. "Patrick needs you," I blurt out.

Sara slides to the edge of the bed and stares at me through tear-soaked eyes. "Is he hurt?" she asks worriedly.

I shake my head no while I reply, "It's Uncle Jack and Sean."

Sara jumps to her feet and bounds up the stairs as I turn to Emma. She is crying uncontrollably, so I sit down next to her on the bed and wrap my arms around her. She is struggling to pull away, but I hold her tight and place my cheek against hers. "It's gonna be OK," I say. "I'll protect you."

Emma puts her hand on my forehead with her thumb pressing against my eye and pushes me backward. It hurts from where she tore the skin off yesterday, so I pull back away from her. "What's going on?" she asks.

"They're here to kill us," I say before once again repeating. "Don't worry, I'll protect you."

She relents a bit but still pushes away from me. "I'm scared and wanna go home." She is sobbing and wriggling to break free, but I continue to hold on to her. I understand she is frightened, and I don't want to see her like that, but I can't believe she is being so mean to me. As I grip her right wrist, she glances a blow off of the top of my head. "I wanna go home!" she repeats, but this time yells it loudly.

I let go and stand up in front of her while scowling. "What for?" I ask. "You wanna go home to those murderers?"

She stops squirming, and stares at me, confused. Her beautiful green eyes are red and watering. Her lovely auburn hair is mussed and covers part of her face. I calm myself while reaching my hand out to brush the hair behind her ear. She cowers but continues to stare at me with a look of uncertainty. "I will take care of you," I declare. "Now be still and I'll come get you when it's clear."

I don't wait for her to respond, as I know she needs a minute. I turn and climb the stairs into the kitchen, closing the door behind me. I peek out the window and see that most of the men are gone, but a few still scurry to the front side of the house. As I enter the living room, I notice Sara is kneeling beside Uncle Jack and Patrick still stands off to the side of the screen door, keeping watch outside. No sign of Sean.

On the floor, Uncle Jack is lying on his side. He is writhing with pain and groans loudly in agony as Sara works on his back to wipe away blood while doing her best to clean the wound. I pick up his jar of moonshine and kneel in front of him. He coughs and hacks as I twist the lid and he smiles a bit as I lift it to his lips. Leaning his head toward the jar, Uncle Jack opens his mouth and allows me to pour the moonshine in. Most of it spills to the floor as he is trying to drink sideways and continually pulls back to cough before returning his face for another swallow. This goes on for a while before he pulls his head all the way back and rests it on the floor.

"Bless you, my boy," he mutters quietly between coughing attacks.

Each time Uncle Jack coughs, a light spray of blood exits his mouth and shoots into the air. He rests his hand in mine and squeezes lightly as Sara continues to work. She still has tear stains on her cheeks, but her sobbing has disappeared. After a few minutes, Sean appears out of the back room with the tommy gun in one hand and rags in the other. He stops next to Sara and extends them out to her. While taking the rags from him, she makes eye contact and shakes her head no. Sean slowly nods his head but says nothing as Sara stuffs the rags under Uncle Jack and rolls him onto his back.

Sean picks up a pillow from the sofa. Kneels down and carefully picks up Uncle Jack's head and places the pillow underneath. Uncle Jack continues to cough but has slowed a little as his breathing has got lighter. Sean rubs his hair and stares into Uncle Jack's eyes. "You're gonna be OK," he says softly.

Uncle Jack smiles up at Sean. "Liar," he replies while wheezing and coughing lightly. "Promise me you'll make 'em pay for what they did."

Sean smiles and nods his head while still rubbing Uncle Jack's head. "You bet your ass we will."

All three of us sit there for a few minutes in silence as Uncle Jack slowly closes his eyes. His chest swells with each shallow, wheezing breath and seems to whistle softly.

"Is he gone?" Patrick asks from the door.

"No," Sean answers as he stands to his feet. "But he doesn't have long."

Sara starts weeping again as she also stands to her feet. She walks over to Sean and places her hand over his wound. "Come on," she says. "Let me take a look at that."

The left side of Sean's shirt is blood soaked and his left arm trembles a bit. He shakes his head no while giving her a little smile for comfort. "It'll be OK," he states. "Bullet went all the way through, and I doctored it a bit myself." He looks down at me. "Pass me that jar, Cieran. That'll help more than anything."

I pick up the jar and stand to my feet while reaching it out to him. He tries to take it with his left hand, but winces and thinks better. Laying his gun on the sofa, he takes the jar in his right hand and holds it steady for me to remove the cap. Sean tilts it to his mouth and swallows heavily as he finishes the rest of the moonshine. He cocks his head to the side, winks his left eye, and blows out through his lips. "Boy, that's good," he declares. "I wish I had some more."

At first, I think about running out to the shed to grab another jar before realizing we are in the middle of a gunfight. I fish my pack of cigarettes out of my pocket and put one in my mouth before offering one to Sean. He takes it from me, and I strike a match, first lighting his and then mine.

"Thank you," he says while picking up the gun off the sofa and disappearing into the kitchen.

"You got one of them for me?" Patrick asks.

I nod and carry him my pack. He leans the shotgun against the wall, and I notice he has the other tommy gun resting next to him against the wall. He must've gotten it while I was in the cellar, I think. Patrick pulls a cigarette out and passes the pack back to me. I look at it and see how crumpled it is from my crushing fall before finally putting it back in my pocket. I try to pass him my matches, but he shakes his head as he pulls a box from his pocket.

I glance out the screen door and see many men moving about and taking cover. I count them before I recognize Dutch's car coming back down the road.

"Dutch is here," I say calmly while glancing back at Patrick.

His mouth falls open as he stares at me in awe. "What the hell!" he exclaims.

It is at this moment that I realize Patrick has not heard that I am talking again. He never asked how I could tell the others about what I'd heard at the Kelleys' since everything happened so quickly and now here, we are.

I smile at him as he stands there, mouth gaping. "Yeah," I say to him. "I can talk."

223

Chapter 12

The Vengeance

As Dutch's car drives down the road, it is flagged to stop by Captain Lewis as he runs toward them. He stands at the back door waving his hands around while pointing toward the house. All the others are still in position with guns fixed toward our home. While scanning the surroundings, my attention stops right off our porch at the slumped body of Evan Blake. A large pool of blood surrounds his head and flies swarm in bunches. I can't help but chuckle to myself while thinking that Dutch had brought in Evan to be his muscle and Sean killed him in a matter of seconds before he even knew that it was coming.

I continue to look around at all the bullet holes and bodies lying about from our gunfight. I turn and look inside the house and realize how badly everything is shot up. I had not really noticed until now. Holes in every wall, the screen door ripped up, glass all over the place. Holding my gaze, I watch as Uncle Jack struggles to breathe. He sort of looks like he is sleeping, but also looks sick.

Sean has returned to the living room and is holding his gun in his right arm with his left dangling at his side. Patrick moves up behind me, focused intently on Dutch's car. I look around for Sara but can't find her anywhere in the living room. I had not noticed her walking out of the room, and I hope she has gone back down to the cellar and is safe.

Off in the distance, I can hear yelling, but I cannot make out what is being said. I watch as Dutch climbs out of the car and stares in our direction. Captain Lewis waves his hands around and is trying to tell him something, but he does not appear to be listening. The fire rises again in my stomach as Bobby Kelley steps out of the other side and walks around to join his father. He also joins Captain Lewis in yelling and hand waving, but still Dutch continues to stare at our front door without acknowledging their presence.

After a few minutes, Dutch pats Bobby on the arm and holds his hand out as if he is telling him to stay put. He walks in our direction, coming down the street before crossing our driveway. Dutch walks slowly but deliberately with his shoulders back and chin raised. Perfect poise, I think to myself. It's as if he has no fear and owns the moment.

Patrick puts his arm on my shoulder and moves me behind him, giving me a little shove at the end. "Here he comes," he says, and appears to be worried.

Sean grabs me by the arm and pulls me back next to him as we stand side by side behind Patrick. "We should kill him as soon as he steps on the porch," Sean mutters.

Patrick turns and looks at him while shaking his head. "No. I can get him to negotiate."

I can see past Patrick a bit on his left side and watch as Dutch stops next to Evan's body and stares at it for a moment. He removes his hat and tilts his head as he appears to pray over him. Then, as if nothing is wrong, he places his hat on his head and climbs the stairs. He stops halfway to the door and glares at Patrick. Folding his hands together and letting them hang in front of him, he speaks. "Patrick. What in the bloody hell is going on?"

Patrick stands in the middle of the doorway with the screen door still closed and I can barely see around him. He grips the handle and barrel of the shotgun as if he is ready to aim and fire. "It got a little out of hand," he replies.

Dutch glances back over his shoulder toward the body of Evan Blake before again turning to face Patrick. "I'll say," he says nonchalantly. "You killed one of my men."

"I've got a dead brother in here and your men killed Crow!" Yells Patrick. "Uncle Jack is shot to hell and barely alive."

"Which brother?" asks Dutch.

"Ryan," Patrick answers.

Dutch shakes his head as his expression softens, and I believe that he genuinely did not like hearing the news about Ryan and Uncle Jack. But just as quick as he softened, he tightens up again and stares at Patrick threateningly. "And my granddaughter?" he asks. "Might she be in there?"

Patrick exhales and tightens up his stare also. "Yeah, she's in here," he admits.

Dutch takes a step toward the door. "Right there is fine," Patrick says while pointing the shotgun through the screen.

"Pat, that's no way to be," Dutch says in response

while also taking a step back and moving his hands to his side. "Is she OK?"

"She's fine," Patrick answers while nodding his head. "She has a stab wound, but they treated it and she'll be alright. Probably needs a doctor, though."

This angers Dutch as he steps forward again but does not quite reach for the door. His face is close to the screen, and I can hear him breathing heavily. "I want to see my granddaughter!" he yells.

Out of the corner of my eye, I see Sean lifting his gun as he grips the handle with his bad arm. I raise mine also but notice that I am aiming at Patrick's back, so I turn to the side a little.

"We'll get to that," Patrick states loudly. "I want to negotiate a trade."

"Who did it, who took her?" asks Dutch with his hollow eyes now open wide.

Without hesitation, Patrick responds. "Does it matter?" he asks. "Does it really matter at this point? Let's work this out and get her home."

Dutch steps back again and inhales deeply. "Very well," he says in agreement. "What do you have in mind?"

"Give me Bobby and you can have the girl," Patrick answers immediately.

Dutch is flabbergasted. The look on his face is pure shock as he places one hand over his chest and glances back down the road. "My son, Bobby?" he asks.

"That's right," answers Patrick. "Your son Bobby."

He looks at Patrick and still appears confused. "What does Bobby have to do with any of this?"

"He killed my parents!" Patrick yells. "And I

want to make him pay for that."

I can hear the anger in his voice as he speaks, and I am proud of him. I do not like the fact that he wants to trade Emma, but I want to see Bobby Kelley killed. I want to do it myself, but it really does not matter.

"That's preposterous!" exclaims Dutch. "Where would you get such an idea?"

Patrick hesitates and seems to calm a little. "My brother overheard him bragging about it," he admits. "Cieran heard him."

Dutch remains in shock as his eyes open even wider and he stares at Patrick in disbelief. "The dummy?" he asks while scoffing. "Why would you take the word of a dummy?"

I feel my ears go hot as the anger swells. I hate being called that.

"He ain't no dummy!" yells Patrick. "Go ask Bobby for yourself if you don't believe me. His face will tell you all you need to know."

Glancing back over his shoulder again and staring down the road toward Bobby, Dutch stands silent for several minutes. He still wears a dumbfounded expression, but it is mixed with his normal, gnarling features as he tries to sort Patrick's words out in his mind.

"Pat," he says at last. "That don't matter none anyways." He steps closer to the screen and narrows his gaze. "You see, you boys have my granddaughter, and I want her back. I would never give my son up, no matter what he's done."

"That's a shame," Patrick responds while shaking his head.

"Aye, it is," Dutch replies. "I really like you

boys." Dutch seems to smirk a bit but still appears daunting. "I have every policeman in the county on my payroll and I will have a hundred men here by nightfall. Now, give me my granddaughter."

Sean backs away from my side, but I don't look at him as I watch Dutch intently. I can't believe what he is saying. I can appreciate his point as I will do anything for my family, but I can't believe he is protecting a murdering piece of trash like Bobby.

Patrick stands his ground. "You're not getting her back, then. We'll fight till the last one of us falls." He hesitates for a moment before continuing. "Maybe your granddaughter doesn't make it out of this alive."

Dutch grits his teeth as he realizes Patrick has the upper hand and I know in an instance that he is not willing to sacrifice his granddaughter. He loves her too much; I think.

"Well, what do you want then?" he asks calmly while shrugging his shoulders. "You can't have Bobby."

Patrick stays quiet for a minute while thinking over his options. "I'll trade her for the life of me and my family," he finally answers. "Give us time to pack up and we'll leave town. You'll never hear from us again."

I am immediately taken aback. I don't like it. I want to kill Bobby Kelley, and I surely will not leave Emma behind. I start to interject as I glance over at Sean for support, but I cannot see him anywhere. I can't hear his footsteps either, I don't know where he is.

"I'll also give you all the shine we have stockpiled," Patrick adds, trying to sweeten the deal. "Has to be a couple hundred gallons at least."

Dutch grins from ear to ear and nods his head. "Now Pat," he replies. "That's how you negotiate." He steps a little closer to the screen door. "You know there's a lot of dead police officers out here, right?"

Patrick looks around and shrugs his shoulders. "So? What's that got to do with this?"

Dutch still smiles as he mutters. "Just because I let you out of here doesn't mean the law won't come lookin' for ya. I know it's already gone out over the wire, so I'm sure it's only a matter of time before the state police get involved."

Shrugging his shoulders for the second time, Patrick responds, "Guess that means we'll have to get this done quickly so we can get on the road." He points around the yard. "Get these men moved out and so we can go."

Dutch shakes his head. "Not a chance," he says. "Of course, I'll have to see her alive before I agree to anything. That much, I'm sure you can agree on."

Patrick nods and opens the screen door for him. "I understand," he answers. "She's in the cellar."

Hesitantly, Dutch steps over the threshold and stops just inside the door. He stares intently at Patrick and then at me before looking around and scanning the room. His eyes hold on Ryan's covered body for a moment before turning his attention to wheezing Uncle Jack. "What a shame," he says peacefully. "I always liked old Jack. He made a fine brew, he did."

I am glaring at him and feel the anger swelling inside. I will not let this trade happen. I think. I'll kill him now and then I'll get Bobby after. Somehow, some way.

Out of nowhere, gunfire erupts from the left side of the house, and all three of us dive to the floor. I drop my rifle. I crawl my way over to Dutch and grip ahold of his shirt as I fumble to get my pistol out of my pocket.

The hammer catches on my trouser pocket and drops to the floor. As I reach out to grab it, I hit it with my hand and cause it to slide away from me before coming to rest near Uncle Jack. Dutch is staring at me wide eyed as I let go of his collar. Patrick climbs to his knees and points his shotgun at Dutch as I crawl back over and pick up my rifle.

The gunfire is continuous as I drop my head and scoot around the floor. I glance out the bottom of the screen door and watch as Sean moves left to right across our yard toward the driveway. Bullets are spraying from the tommy gun as he moves with the purpose of a soldier fighting in war.

"It's Sean!" I scream.

Patrick's head whips around toward me with a look of desperation covering his face. "Watch Dutch," he yells as he jumps to his feet and runs toward the door.

I climb to my knees and point my rifle at Dutch while still keeping my attention focused on Patrick as he carries the shotgun in one hand and scoops up his tommy gun with the other. He is already lifting the tommy gun as he bursts through the door and starts firing on his way down the steps, meeting Sean just off the front porch near the driveway.

I glance back at Dutch to see that he has rolled to his back and has his hands near his face. He is still wide eyed as he stares at me. A stray bullet burst through the window and thumps loudly as it contacts the wall, spraying plaster into the air. I rise to my feet and slide back inside the doorway while watching out the screen as Sean and Patrick march in unison down the driveway, firing at everything they see.

"I'm out," Sean yells as he kneels down to one

knee. I recognize my father's satchel as he reaches back and pulls out another magazine and reloads while Patrick continues firing by his side. Once clipped, Sean stands and the two of them take off to the right, down the road and out of my sight.

Looking toward the sofa, I plan to move to the other side of the door against the wall so I can watch them, but have to duck as bullets pierce the screen and whizz by my face before striking the wall behind me. A second bullet burst through the back of the couch, blowing cotton into the air as it comes dangerously close to Dutch before hitting Uncle Jack directly in the stomach.

Uncle Jack's body lurches as the bullet penetrates his skin, and he groans loudly. His eyes remain closed while he gingerly squirms in place. I take off toward him and slide to a halt on my knees. I put my hand over his stomach and feel the warmth as blood soaks into my palm. His breathing is shallow, and his wheezing is now mixed with painful, light moaning.

Turning to look at Dutch, I grip my rifle tight. He has turned to his side with his back against the bottom of the sofa and is covering his face with his elbow. Another bullet bursts through the window, cutting through the curtains and blowing them in the air before striking the piano behind me. A loud crack followed by a high-pitched ding ring out, causing me to drop my head to the floor directly next to Uncle Jack's face.

"It'll be OK, Uncle Jack," I blurt out. I don't know why I said it, it just came out and I watch as he opens his eyes slowly and stares at me. He blinks twice before locking eyes with me and gazes deep into my soul. His mouth opens slowly into a smile before he winks his eye weakly at me and he gasps his last breath of air. I lay there for a moment and watch as the light fades from his open eyes and his mouth slowly turns droll before falling open. I can feel my heart wrenching from the loss of such a good man. Lifting my hand to his face, I close his eyes and whisper, "I love you, Uncle Jack."

Another bullet rips through the screen door and strikes the wall off to my right. I don't lift my head, I just lay there for another minute holding Uncle Jack, not wanting to let him go. I hear yelling outside as one of the tommy guns stops firing, then the other.

I slide to the door and peek around the corner. Both Sean and Patrick are walking toward Dutch's car, and I can see Captain Lewis, Bobby Kelley, and a third man positioned behind the car and all three are shooting back. Patrick no longer carries the tommy gun and is steadily firing a shotgun at the three men.

Sean splits off to the left and steps around a parked automobile. His tommy gun stops firing, so he throws it to the ground and pulls a rifle off of his shoulder. As he grips the gun, a man steps out behind him and takes aim. Frantically, I yell out, "behind you!"

He must have heard me as he spins around quickly and fires at the man, hitting him once before shooting him a second time as he drops to the ground. Sean takes a moment to scan the area for other men before turning back toward Dutch's car. I am horrified to see Captain Lewis and the unknown man stepping out in unison toward Sean. Before I can yell, they fire their pistols at him, causing his body to drop to the ground. Sean turns while on his back and fires a shot at Captain Lewis, hitting him in the shoulder and dropping him to the ground. He then takes aim at the other man as a bullet strikes the ground next to him, spraying dirt in the air. Sean pulls the trigger and moments later the man's head flies backward, splattering blood as the man drops to his knees and plunges to the ground.

Captain Lewis is crawling on his knees back toward the automobile as Sean struggles to his feet. He holds one hand to his neck as he walks up behind Captain Lewis and uses his foot to push him to the ground. When he rolls to his back, Sean lifts his rifle and shoots him in the face. He stands there for a moment looking down on Captain Lewis before finally turning toward Patrick.

Patrick has ducked behind a tree as Bobby Kelley fires at him from the cover of the automobile. I am vigorously searching for anyone sneaking up on them and ready my rifle to shoot if needed. Turning my attention back to Sean, I painfully watch as he takes two steps toward Patrick before dropping to his knees. His gun falls to the ground as he clutches his neck with both hands.

"Sean!" I yell out. I open the screen door and step out onto the porch. I am just about to take off toward him when I see Patrick run to his side, dodging bullets from Bobby as he goes.

I lift my rifle and fire toward Bobby. The bullet misses and strikes dirt fifteen feet behind him. Patrick kneels beside Sean and fires a shot back at Bobby, hitting the automobile in the front end and nowhere near him. I steady my gun, close one eye and peer through the sights. Exhaling softly, I squeeze the trigger and watch as my bullet strikes the back of the automobile, narrowly missing Bobby's face by inches. Frightened from not knowing where the shot came from, he immediately jumps to the ground behind the automobile and disappears out of my sight.

Patrick places Sean's arm around his neck and grips him around the waist. Standing up, he points his shotgun with one arm toward Bobby. Without seeing him, he turns and lumbers the two of them toward the house. Sean is able to move his legs but still clutches his neck with his free hand. Patrick grits his teeth, contorting his face and showing sheer determination as he hastily makes his way toward the house with Sean in tow.

Clutching my rifle, I survey the area while constantly looking back toward Bobby Kelley. Nothing, no one moves, and I wonder if we have killed them all. I keep constant watch as Patrick and Sean make their way down the driveway and up the stairs. Sean's head is lowered and bouncing. I notice a bloody wound on his stomach, along with blood seeping around his hand as he holds his neck. They run past me and fall to the floor just inside the door and next to Ryan's deceased body.

"Sara!" Patrick frantically yells out. He sits Sean up and fumbles with his shirt before once again yelling out. "Sara, I need your help!"

I can hear her footsteps running up the stairs and as I turn to look toward the kitchen, I notice Dutch has moved next to Uncle Jack and is using his body as a shield. Sara rounds the corner from the kitchen and stares in the direction of Patrick and Sean. Tears are streaming down her cheeks, and she wears an expression of sheer terror. Without hesitation, she runs to their side and kneels next to Sean.

"He's hurt bad!" Patrick exclaims.

Sara places her hand over Sean's at his neck and

pulls it away. Blood spurts out and Sean looks as if he is going to pass out. His eyelids narrow as his body sways back and forth, with Patrick holding on and trying his best to stabilize him.

"Oh, lord," Sara cries out as she grabs one of the rags next to Ryan and places it on his neck.

"Bobby, get in here!"

My head whirls toward Dutch and I am horrified to see that he is on his knees and has my pistol pointed at Patrick. He is snarling with eyes narrow as he instantly fires a shot, hitting Patrick in the forehead, causing his body to slump to the floor.

"No!" Sara yells out while reaching toward Patrick.

Dutch turns slightly and fires a shot at Sara, hitting her on the left side of her chest. Blood flies as her small body is violently thrust backward. As her head hits the floor, he fires a second shot directly into her temple. Her head rolls slightly back and forth before coming to a rest with her eyes wide open.

I lift my rifle and roll to my right as Dutch fires a shot at me, narrowly missing and striking the floor next to my shoulder. I stretch out and point my rifle at him. Without taking aim, I pull the trigger and watch as his head whips backward. His body quickly follows, and he comes to rest while laying on top of Uncle Jack's body. I try to fire a second shot, just to be sure and kill him, but hear only a click and know that I am out of bullets.

Glancing back at Sean, I see he is crawling toward me. Before I can move, I hear footsteps coming up the stairs before stopping just outside the door.

"Dad!" the voice calls out. "I'm comin' in."

The sound sends shivers down my spine as I

know it is Bobby Kelley. I immediately slump my body and lay silently still. Hesitantly, he opens the screen door slowly. Before stepping inside, he sees Sean crawling and fires a shot, striking Sean in the back. Sean groans loudly and writhes in pain.

With his attention focusing on Sean, Bobby walks through the door and steps over me with the heel of his foot touching my body. How fitting, I think to myself. This is the exact spot that he hit me in the head and left me for dead.

I can hear my heart pounding through my ears as I climb upward and, with one motion, pull my knife out of its sheath and stab him in the back of the calf. He yells out in pain as he falls to one knee. He turns and swings his pistol toward me. I catch it with my left hand while swinging mightily with my right, burying my knife in the middle of his back. The pistol falls from his grasp as he slumps to the floor on his side. He cries out in agony as I struggle to pull the knife from his flesh. While wiggling and pulling, I get it dislodged and roll him over and onto his back. As I climb on top of him, I straddle him with both legs as he claws at my face and tries to push me off.

"No!" he yells out in terror as I lift the knife over my head and grab on with both hands.

"Yes!" I roar while using every ounce of my power to drive the knife down and into his chest.

His eyes go wide with shock and horror as his mouth gapes open. His hands are over mine as I sit there for a moment while holding the knife in his flesh and glare down into his eyes. I speak no words, just stare deep into his soul, hoping he understands. I feel jubilation as his hands fall limp and his eyes lose their luster. I have done it. I have killed Bobby Kelley!

A few moments pass after he drew his last breath, yet I continue to sit on top of him. My heart is racing and my chest heaves as I gulp air while open mouthed. I am relieved, and it feels good. As my rage dissipates and I come back to reality, I glance over at Sean to find him lying on the floor open eyed and smiling at me.

I climb off Bobby and crawl over to him. He is grunting through irregular breaths. As I roll him over to his back, he groans softly but never moves his arms. Blood streams from his neck and I can see jagged skin where the bullet had torn through. I reach out and pick the rag up off the floor, pressing it over the wound. Glancing down, I frantically pull his shirt up to find a large hole seeping blood. I know Bobby shot him in the back and in the shoulder earlier. I smile as I lock eyes with him again.

"You're a tough son of a bitch," I say softly.

Managing a meager smile, Sean mumbles something to me that I cannot understand as his head sags to the side, and he exhales one last time.

Exhausted, I stare at Sean for a moment before looking around the room at everyone as they lay dead around me. Tears form in the corner of my eyes as the realization sets in that they have died because of me. They died protecting me. I look at Bobby, then over at Dutch as he lays back on Uncle Jack's torso. I can't believe I let him get to my gun and kill Patrick and Sara. I feel the anger swell back up as I think about it. This time, it is me I am angry with. They would still be here if only I had kept watch over him better. That's what Patrick told me to do was watch him and I had failed.

I am quickly drawn back to the moment as

anxiety replaces my anger. How many men are still out there, I wonder? How many are coming? I get up and look out the door. Nothing moves and not a sound other than the wind blowing along the bushes. I turn around and glance across the room, spotting the box with the money in it. Sean still has my satchel, so I wiggle it from around his shoulder and wipe away what blood I can. Kneeling beside the box, I briskly scoop the money and stuff it in the satchel. I grab a box of shotgun shells and collect the shotgun laying next to Patrick's body while being careful not to disturb it as I step over him. Walking to the kitchen, I spot my pistol lying next to Dutch and grab it, stuffing it in the satchel and close the hasp. As I stand there looking down at Dutch's dead body, I notice his expression is no longer as grim as I remember. He just looks like an old man. I smile to myself as I reach into my pocket and pull out the folded-up photo of Emma.

"This is the only way you can have your granddaughter now," I say aloud as I lay it in his open hand.

Opening the cellar door, I feel excited, as I cannot wait to see Emma. I bound down the stairs and cross the floor, coming to a stop at the edge of her bed. Emma is huddled in the corner of the bed with her knees up to her chin and has her arms wrapped around her legs. She is quivering wildly. Her whole body shakes and she appears horrified. I feel terrible for her as I think about all the shooting upstairs and must have scared her badly. I reach my hand out to her and watch as she tightens up before burying her head in her knees.

Looking down at my hand, I realize I am covered in blood. Both hands, my arms, my clothing, all covered.

I walk over to the bedside table and lean the shotgun against the wall. I dip my hands in the water basin and clean as fast as I can. As I rub each hand and forearm, the water turns from pink to a deeper red. Even though I still have bloodstains on my arms, I dry off quickly and pick up the shotgun. While reaching my free hand out for Emma's, I say to her. "Come on, we have to go."

She still looks afraid, and I see tears welling up in her eyes once again as she hesitantly takes my hand in hers before sliding to the edge of the bed and standing up. The nightgown that Sara had given her fits a little big, but I am amazed at how beautiful she is and I smile widely at her. I take only a moment to bask in her beauty before urgently pulling her toward the stairs.

Her legs are shaky, but she can climb the steps as I pull her from above. At the door, I stop and listen for a moment. With no sound coming from the other room, I step out into the kitchen and walk toward the back door.

"Where are we going?" asks Emma as I let go of her hand to twist the knob.

I again take her hand while using my shoulder to push open the screen door before stepping out on the back porch. I hesitate for a minute as I look all around, searching for movement. After seeing nothing, I take off down the steps, pulling Emma as I go. At the bottom, she trips and falls to her knees, groaning. I never let go of her hand and lift as she lumbers to her feet before taking off again toward the shed.

"Where are we going?" she asks again as I let go of her hand to open the doors.

"Away from here," I reply, focused on my task.

Reaching back for her hand and not finding it, I turn to look at her. She is inching away from me and crying hysterically. "Come on," I say politely. "There will be people coming."

She starts to run, but I grab her and wrap my arm around her stomach, dragging her toward the truck. She is kicking and screaming, and I don't understand why she fights me. "Stop it," I say sternly. "We don't have time for this."

Once we reach the truck, I push her toward the driver's side but must have pushed too hard as she falls to the ground with a wallop. I slide the shotgun in bed under the tarp and reach down for her. She slaps my hand away, so I grab onto her with both hands, pick her up, and push her into the seat. I slip the satchel from around my neck and reach inside, pulling out my pistol. Emma immediately slides to the passenger side as I toss the satchel in the seat and climb in, tucking the pistol under my leg.

It takes a few tries before the truck finally starts. I put it into gear and ease out of the shed. Turning left and cutting through the yard, I step on the pedal as I already know where I am going.

Following the road to the left, I make my way through the bottoms as fast as I can drive. I keep constant watch behind me but find it difficult, as I am not a very good driver yet. Emma's body sloshes back and forth across the cab with her moaning at each bump. I can hear the liquor bottles clanking in the back and don't want to break them, but I know I don't have a lot of time to get away. I turn right up into the hills, heading for an old mining cabin that my father used to bring us to when we were hunting. He said it was where the foreman used to stay when the hills were being mined. It is quite a ways up in the hills and few people know about it, so it will be the perfect place to hang low until nightfall so I can get us out of town.

The drive to the cabin takes around twenty minutes as we twist and turn our way through the hills. I have not seen a single person along the way, but that was not odd at this time of year. Not much going on in the hills. Has a few decent streams for fishing but it is good hunting in the winter.

I slow a little as I search for the driveway to the cabin. I know it is around here somewhere, but there is no real marker for it and cannot be seen from the road. A few years back, Patrick drove a stake out by the road and painted the tip brown. I slow down even more to almost a crawl as I feel like we are close and sure enough, there it is. The driveway is overgrown with weeds and has narrowed from tree limb growth on both sides. They scrape the side of the truck as I drive through, creating a screeching sound heard over the engine. Once I am a little way off the road, I set the brake and jump out, putting my pistol in my pocket. I do not intend to make the same mistake I had at Crow's. This time, I go back and use a broken tree limb to cover my tracks. Cannot even tell that I drove through here, I think.

I jump back in the cab and continue down the driveway. The area is heavily wooded, but eventually opens up and the cabin is visible. It's not much to look at and it might have worn a little more since we were up here last winter, I believe. The windows are all busted out and the roof leaks badly, but it has a fireplace and is a decent place to get in out of the cold wind. A lot of good memories here, I think to myself. Me and my brothers and my father all hanging out here goofing around and telling stories. I'm going to miss them all.

Pulling up next to the cabin, I cut the engine off, grab the satchel and step out. I pull the shotgun out of the bed and walk around to the passenger side. After opening the door, I hold my hand out for Emma's. Hesitantly, she takes it and steps her bare feet down on the rocky grass. It is a slow walk with sticks and stones everywhere as Emma hobbles and winces each time she takes a step. Once inside, I look around the small, one-room cabin and notice that it is just as we had left it. Empty, all except for a small, makeshift table with one chair on the left side and a fireplace with a few pieces of wood on the right side. There used to be a little wooden bed, but we busted it up and burnt it one year. Dad said he was tired of us fighting over who would sleep in the bed and that now we can all sleep on the floor together.

I lay the satchel on the table and lean the shotgun against the wall. Looking at Emma, I say, "there's a little stream on the back side. Let's go clean up."

She still stares at me oddly and is making me uncomfortable. "What are we doing here?" she asks as she chokes back tears.

I walk over and take her by the hand before leading her back out the door. "Gonna wait it out here until nightfall," I say, while trying to comfort her. "It'll be safer to travel at night."

As we walk around the back toward the stream, she asks, "Then where are we going?"

I shrug my shoulders before responding. "Not sure yet, but I'm thinking Kansas City. Got some family up there."

I don't know where they live, but I am sure I can find them. While leaning down, I dip my hands in the stream and wipe my face. The water is cool and feels good. I lean down and take a long drink before glancing back at Emma as she stands there watching me.

"Aren't you gonna clean up a little?" I ask.

She shakes her head no and folds her hands in front of her.

"Do you wanna drink?" I ask, while trying to make conversation. "It's gonna be awhile until we get somewhere to get a drink."

Again she shakes her head no. "I wanna go home," she mutters as her voice cracks and tears well in her eyes.

"Can't right now," I reply, trying to be patient. "But you're with me now and I'll take care of you."

I take my shirt off and dunk it into the water. While using it as a rag, I wipe my face, arms, hands, and upper body before dunking it back in the water and scrubbing it against itself to try to clean it. My trousers and even my socks have blood all over them, but I am content with just cleaning my shirt. I'll worry about the others later, I think. Plus, I need to get Emma some clothes and a pair of shoes.

Once I am satisfied with the cleanliness of my shirt, I wring it out and start back toward the cabin. Emma stands there for a minute, watching water flow over the rocks and seems content with the beauty of it.

"You coming?" I ask after a few minutes.

Slowly, she turns her head toward me and her body soon follows as we walk back to the cabin. I lay my shirt over the hood of the truck to allow it to dry in the sunlight before we both walk inside. I motion for her to sit in the chair as I pick up the shotgun and satchel. Walking to the other side of the room, I slide down the wall and come to rest on the floor. It feels good to sit and relax, I think. I pull the pistol out of my pocket and open the satchel, feeling around for the bullets I'd put in earlier. I find some and pull out a handful, laying them on my lap. I open the revolver and pull out the four empty shells before tossing them toward the fireplace. Emma's head whips toward the sound and she sits there, watching as I reload the pistol and put the remaining bullets back in the satchel. Once finished, I put the pistol back in my pocket and load up the shotgun before placing it on the floor beside me.

With nothing else to do, I breathe in deeply and try to relax. It is going to be awhile until nightfall, and I need to calm myself. What a big day, I think. I feel the sadness wash over me as I relive each one of my family members' deaths, even Crow. I am going to miss them all very much. I think back to the shootout and how it made me feel. How electric and exciting it was! I think about shooting Dutch and about being able to kill Bobby Kelley. I like the fact that I was able to get him with a knife. It makes it a little more personable to me. After a while, I realize I am smiling as I stare back up at Emma. She is leaned back in the chair and is staring out the window. The sunlight shines on her face and gleams through her auburn hair as wind gusts from the open window, blowing her hair to the side. She is beautiful and now she is mine. I will do everything in my power to make her happy. We have money and a little moonshine to sell. Maybe I can start my own still, I wonder. We can get married and be happy. Of course, I know it is going to take time, and she still isn't very friendly to me. But I will make her love me.

We sat there in silence for several hours, neither of us speaking to the other. I do not know what to say to her and I guess she feels the same. Every so often, one of us would get up and walk around the room to stretch our legs as the other one would watch. I had to step out to use the restroom once, and I wondered if she needed to also, but I never asked. I figured she would say something if she had to.

Once the sun goes down, I pace around the room as my anxiety grows within me. I am ready to get out of here and ready to settle in somewhere. As soon as I see the sun sink out of the sky and night settle upon us, I grab the shotgun and satchel and head for the truck. "Let's get out of here," I say excitedly.

I am halfway to the truck before I realize Emma has not followed me. I go back inside, and she is standing just inside the door and watching me curiously.

"Are you coming?" I ask as I reach my hand for hers.

Tears start streaming down her face as she hesitantly takes my hand and joins me on the walk to the truck. I open the door and help her inside. "It's gonna be alright," I say as I pat her on the leg affectionately.

She only stares blankly back at me and does not respond, so I close the door and run around the truck, securing the shotgun in the back before opening the door and jumping in. I can feel it as I start the engine and back up to turn the truck toward the driveway. My heart is racing and I am excited. I turn on the headlamps and put the truck in gear. Lurching forward, I drive us back down the driveway. At the road, I turn left and decide my best way is to go the back way out of the hills and to put some distance between us and my house. I know it is a much slower road but safer to travel. We curve and slide around road after road until finally we arrive at a blacktop intersection. I'm not sure how to get to Kansas City, but I am fairly certain that the left is north, so I pull out and take off that way. I feel something poking me in my leg, so I reach in my pocket and pull out my pistol. I turn it over in my hand a few times, admiring its beauty before laying it to rest on the seat between Emma and I.

My heart dances in my chest as I shift gears. Nervously, I pull a cigarette from the pouch and strike a match. I can't help but notice my hands are shaking uncontrollably. It's not fear that consumes me, it's anxiety. With each draw from the cigarette, I can feel myself starting to calm. I stare out the windshield, watching the beams graze the road. The hum of the engine, the rattle of the cargo I haul. It is intoxicating. I am alive and feel the anxiousness rise again. I know my life is forever changed.

After twenty minutes, I notice a filling station along the side of the road and pull in. I grab a couple of dollars out of the satchel and run inside. I gaze around for a moment before finding a cooler and pull out a couple of Cokes. Walking to the register, I see a pack of jerky and lay it on the counter with the Cokes. The man behind the register stares at me with bewilderment as I stand in front of him.

"That all?" he asks, while narrowing his eyes at me.

"Gonna need a fill up," I reply. Glancing up at the man, I ask. "How do you get to Kansas City?"

The man stares at me for a moment before pointing out the window. "Straight up that road," he answers. "For another hundred mile or so. Then you got to do some turning. Got a map over there if you need it."

I turn to look where he points his finger before walking over to a small table. It is a map of the whole state of Missouri, so I pick it up and take it back to the register. I don't know how to read a map, but I'll figure it out; I think. I lay two dollars on the counter and pick up the sodas and jerky.

The man picks up the money and stares at it. "That's not enough for a fill up, son," he says.

I nod and feel a little embarrassed. "Just give me whatever that'll get me," I say before turning and walking out the door.

I hear the bell ring on the door behind me as I climb in the seat and know he is on his way.

"I got us some Cokes and jerky," I say as I reach out to hand one of the Cokes to Emma.

She doesn't take it from me, so I turn to face her. She has both hands on my pistol with the hammer cocked and is pointing it at me. Her eyes narrow as she glares down the wobbling barrel, created by her trembling hands with eyes pouring tears. I reach the bottle up a little higher toward her.

"Here," I say playfully, while smiling at her. "Put that thing away."

My right ear rings out and heat consumes my cheek as the first shot bursts through the bottle and slams into my jaw. My head flies backward violently and I see nothing but darkness as the second shot hits me in the chest. My eyesight returns a little as I lift my body forward and place a hand on my cheek. Bewildered, I watch as Emma grits her teeth while muttering something before firing a third shot. The pain is unbearable as I slump over and rest my face on the steering wheel. I can feel blood running down my neck and I feel the burning in my chest as I gasp for air. My ears ring loudly, and I struggle to catch my thoughts. I lay there against the steering wheel, staring at Emma as her hands tremble and smoke dissipates from the barrel of the gun. All the anger is gone from her face as she is crying, and tears pour down her cheeks. My goodness, I think to myself, isn't she beautiful!?

Chapter 13

The Epilogue

I wonder where he's taking me; I think to myself as he gets out of the truck and goes inside. I need to use the restroom, and I want to go home. I want my mom and dad. I wonder if I can run away. I don't see any houses around, but I see a man standing up through the window at the service station and wonder if he can save me. Cieran is covered in blood and will surely kill the man before he can help me. I put my hand down on the seat to help as I change positions and feel the cold metal on my palm. Picking it up, I am surprised to realize he has forgotten his gun. I look around, not knowing what to do. If I run, I can shoot at him if he chases me, I think. Oh god, here he comes, I worry. I don't even know how to shoot this thing. I use my thumb to pull back the hammer. Just aim and shoot, I tell myself.

My hands shake uncontrollably and my heart races as he climbs into the seat next to me. I aim the gun at his head as he says something to me, but I'm not able to pay attention. As he glances at me, his eyes glow with darkness, and I can see there is something evil deep in his soul. Afraid, I squeeze the trigger and jump at the sound of the explosion. The gun almost falls from my hand as I cock the hammer again and shoot a second time. Blood is already streaming from his face and the second shot hurt him badly. I cock the hammer again and fire once more. He slumps over the steering wheel, and I watch as he blinks his cold dead eyes while smiling at me.

Dropping the gun, I fidget with the door handle before finally getting it open and falling outside to the ground.

"Somebody help me," I yell hysterically as I crawl toward the back of the truck. "He's crazy!"

In 1980, I was born in Joplin, Missouri to Shirley Jean and Freddy Dean Rickey where I had a formidable childhood, traveling place to place and only staying put for a short period of time. I loved my parents very much but unfortunately lost both of them in a tragic turn of events at the age of ten. Following their death, my sisters and I went to live with my aunt and uncle in an underprivileged part of town. I struggled through my adolescence as I failed to deal with the death of my parents, poverty, and loneliness as I tried to find my way in this world.

At the age of seventeen, I met the love of my life, Shelley and unfortunately dropped out of school not long after so that I could work to earn a living. I traveled the country doing construction but was unable to deny my demons, which created many obstacles for her and I. Finally, at the age of twenty-two, I met the second love of my life when my wife gave birth to our daughter, Morgan. Understanding that I could not raise a child properly with the life I was living, I took a job at a pet food manufacturing plant working overnight weekends in an entry level position. Over the next fifteen years, I worked extremely hard and under the leadership of great mentors, I was able to work my way up and eventually became the Operations Manager over the entire facility.

Satisfied with my success, I decided it was time for me to make a change and try something different in life. During a two-week quarantine with Covid, I purchased a restaurant and opened a new chapter of my life. During the course of three years, I met some lifelong friends and found enjoyment with serving others. Unfortunately, I continued to struggle with my demons and found myself drinking heavily while working unbearably long hours to keep the restaurant afloat. On the third year, having gained a considerable amount of weight, facing paramount stress as well as overindulgence; I had a heart attack. Having enough, my wife made me sell the restaurant and take a couple months off to relax. On day two of sitting around the house and while facing my own mortality, I decided that I wanted to leave something for my daughter and her children to remember me by. I sat down at a rickety old desk and over the next couple months, Beautiful; Crazy was born.

I now own an antique store at the edge of town and find absolute happiness in searching for old treasures. I enjoy spending time with my friends and family and do my best to spoil my two dogs, Jolene and Maggie May. I have struggled with addiction. I have struggled with depression and suicide. I have struggled with poverty. I have struggled with loneliness. I have struggled to fit in. I have laughed and I have cried. I have been happy, and I have been sad. I have loved and I have lost. I am no different than anyone else in this world! I do not know what the future holds for any of us, but I do know that if we lay the foundation for happiness, it is just within our reach!

Made in the USA
Coppell, TX
24 January 2025

44910666R00152